"My cell pho
card, so please
your cousin h
you might

Laurel forced a laugh. "Of course not. We're perfectly safe."

But considering the telephone call and the letter in her purse, Laurel hoped her optimistic words had disguised her inner turmoil from her daughter Debbie and from Michah.

"Cousin Kevin is a worrywart," Debbie said. "We have nothing to fear from our neighbors, and travelers wouldn't know there's a house out here."

"But you *are* isolated," Michah insisted, "so please contact me if you need anything. I'll be here almost every night."

Michah's eyes revealed a warm tenderness and concern that made Laurel's heart beat faster. Knowing his strength and intelligence were at her beck and call gave her the assurance that she desperately needed.

Books by Irene Brand

Love Inspired

Child of Her Heart #19
Heiress #37
To Love and Honor #49
A Groom To Come
   Home To #70
Tender Love #95
The Test of Love #114

Autumn's Awakening #129
Summer's Promise #148
*Love at Last #190
*Song of Her Heart #200
*The Christmas Children #234
*Second Chance at Love #244
*Listen to Your Heart #280

*The Mellow Years

IRENE BRAND

Writing has been a lifelong interest of this author, who says that she started her first novel when she was eleven years old and hasn't finished it yet. However, since 1984 she's published thirty-two contemporary and historical novels and three nonfiction titles. She started writing professionally in 1977 after she completed her master's degree in history at Marshall University. Irene taught in secondary public schools for twenty-three years, but retired in 1989 to devote herself to writing.

Consistent involvement in the activities of her local church has been a source of inspiration for Irene's work. Traveling with her husband, Rod, to all fifty states, and to thirty-two foreign countries has also inspired her writing. Irene is grateful to the many readers who have written to say that her inspiring stories and compelling portrayals of characters with strong faith have made a positive impression on their lives. You can write to her at P.O. Box 2770, Southside, WV 25187 or visit her Web site at www.irenebrand.com.

LISTEN TO
YOUR HEART

IRENE BRAND

Steeple
Hill®

Published by Steeple Hill Books™

STEEPLE HILL BOOKS

Steeple
Hill®

ISBN 0-373-87290-9

LISTEN TO YOUR HEART

www.SteepleHill.com

Printed in U.S.A.

But the Lord is faithful, and He will strengthen
and protect you from the evil one.
—*II Thessalonians* 3:3

Chapter One

Persistent rain drummed a staccato rhythm on the tin roof of the back porch as Laurel Cooper leaned a ladder against the outside wall of her Tennessee antebellum home.

"There would have to be another downpour before that lazy contractor got here," Laurel fumed. She tied her raincoat's hood over her red hair and climbed the ladder. Laurel shook her fist at an offending eaves spout, which, rather than draining as it should, was spewing water into her favorite bed of hostas.

Laurel had learned to do a lot of things since she'd been the owner of Oaklawn, but this was the first time she'd tackled a leak in the middle of a thunderstorm. The raincoat provided some protection from the torrent as she took a hammer out of one of her pockets, stuck some nails in her mouth and leaned toward a metal strap that had broken and caused the gutter to separate.

She scowled at several miniature ponds in her land-scaping. With all of these delays, how could she possibly beautify Oaklawn in time for Debbie's August wedding just three months from now?

Believing she was alone, Laurel almost fell off the ladder when a loud knock sounded at the nearby door. Recovering her balance, she peered through the screened back porch. Protected by a large umbrella, a man stood at the door.

"It's high time you got here," Laurel shouted above a roll of thunder. "I've been waiting two days for you to come and do what should have been done weeks ago."

"I beg your pardon," the man said.

"And so you should," Laurel answered crossly. "My hostas are about ruined. Come and fix this leak."

He left the doorstep and walked languidly toward her. She didn't recognize him, but the contractor who'd renovated her home employed a lot of people. She'd seen many different workers during the renovation. As this man approached, Laurel backed down the ladder. She extended the hammer and nails to him, irritated that a workman would appear on her doorstep empty-handed.

A smile seemed to lurk at the corners of his mouth, but his vivid blue eyes were unfathomable. He laid aside the umbrella, took the hammer and nails and obediently climbed the ladder. "It isn't funny!" Laurel said angrily. "I spent more money than I can afford on this project, and this is the fourth time I've had to have one of your workers redo something."

The workman winced when a spurt of water splashed his face and drenched the front of his shirt.

Laurel bit her lips to stifle further comments, since her conscience hurt a little because the man was getting soaked. Maybe she should have delayed the repair until the rain was over, but she couldn't afford to replace the plants. Besides, why would he come to work on a day like this dressed only in a cotton shirt and dress trousers? And without any tools? She knew reliable workers were hard to find, but this was ridiculous!

With a few deft movements, the man squeezed the guttering together, pounded three nails in the brace that held the guttering to the building, and the leak was fixed. Still atop the ladder, he turned and said, "Is the work satisfactory now, ma'am?"

His long, thick black hair, dusted with gray, was plastered to his head. Compelling blue eyes gleamed from his square, tanned face. He wasn't a particularly handsome man, but his clinging wet clothes revealed a tall, rugged, perfectly proportioned body. Why did she have the feeling he was laughing at her?

Laurel realized she'd been staring at the man when he prodded, "If the work suits you, I'd like to find a drier place. I'm reminded of my dad's expression about people who didn't know enough to come in out of the rain."

Annoyed because of his suspected levity, Laurel answered tartly, "As long as the water is going down the gutter, it's okay. I'm sorry you got wet, but you should know better than to come to work on a day like this without a raincoat. Come inside, there's something else I want you to do."

Micah Davidson stepped down and handed the hammer to Laurel. He shouldered the ladder and set it on the porch, then picked up his umbrella and joined her. His humor at the situation was tempered by the fact that he was drenched.

"Ma'am," he said, "let me introduce myself—"

"This way," Laurel said, and motioned imperiously. He followed her into the broad entryway of the palatial mansion. She untied the hood, shrugged out of her raincoat and hung it on the rack by the door.

Micah's eyes widened appreciably. The woman's red hair, with tints of reddish gold, clung to her head in short curls. She had alabaster skin and a petite body, giving her an appearance of fragile beauty. Judging by the way she'd been bossing him around, she certainly wasn't frail. Her green eyes flashed like neon lights when she was angry, and he thought humorously that, with her red hair and green eyes, her head would make a good Christmas tree ornament. He still had no idea who she was.

Laurel placed her right foot on the bottom step of the curved, hanging stairway in the central hall. The board wiggled back and forth beneath her sturdy white shoes.

"That board hasn't been nailed down, and it's an accident waiting to happen. My daughter tripped on it last week."

Micah's lips twitched as he said, "I'll have to borrow your hammer again. And maybe a nail or two."

"Just a minute!" Laurel said, suspicion dawning in her mind. "Why'd you come to work without any tools? Aren't you from Bowman's Contractors?"

"No, ma'am."

Because of a sudden flash of embarrassment, Laurel's temper flared again, and she said, "Why didn't you say so?"

"I tried to, ma'am."

"Oh, stop calling me ma'am. My name is Laurel Cooper. Who are you anyway?"

"Micah Davidson."

"What's your business here?"

He reached into his damp pants pocket, pulled out a leather case and handed her a business card.

"Micah Davidson—Photojournalist," she read in a subdued voice. Laurel turned away from him and covered her face with both hands. He sensed she was close to tears.

"My miserable temper is always getting me into trouble," she confessed in a muffled voice. "I'm so humiliated. Please go away, Mr. Davidson, and save me further embarrassment." She turned toward him with downcast eyes peeking out over her hands. "Although I suppose I should be polite enough to ask what brought you to Oaklawn."

"I noticed a sign along the highway indicating you have apartments for rent. I have an assignment in this area and I need a place to live for a few weeks."

Still refusing to meet his eyes, she stared at the floor.

"Would you like to come back later when you have dry clothing? I'm sure you must be miserable."

"My luggage is in the car. If I can rent one of your apartments, I'll have a place to change my clothes. Do you have anything available?"

"I have a vacant upstairs apartment. The central part of the house was built in 1830, but a two-story ell was added around 1900. I had that wing converted into four apartments when I inherited this house two years ago. They're modern and quite comfortable. Come with me, and I'll let you see the rooms. Most of my renters are students at nearby Walden College and are on summer break now. I hold their rooms for them through the summer at a reduced rate."

Laurel motioned him to follow her through the rear door into a large flower garden, bordered by a white wooden fence. The thunderstorm had passed, leaving a moist, fragrant scent to the newly mowed grass. Drops of moisture decorated dozens of rosebushes, enhancing the sweet aroma of the flowering buds. An industrious robin pulled a fat worm from the damp ground and hopped across the wet grass to feed her fledgling offspring. Micah surveyed his surroundings with pleasure. For years he'd rambled around the world with no place to call home. Why did he now experience the comfortable peace of belonging?

"I'm on assignment to photograph and write an article on antebellum homes in Tennessee and Kentucky," Micah explained, "and Oaklawn is one of the houses on my list. I hope you'll let me feature your home in my article."

Laurel slanted a glance his way. His deep voice contained a pleasant hint of huskiness. "That would be wonderful! This house has been in my husband's family for generations. I'm often overwhelmed by its vastness, but it's my daughter's heritage, and I'm trying to maintain it for her."

Micah discreetly glanced at Laurel's hands. Seeing no wedding band, he decided she must be a widow, or she wouldn't have been the one to inherit the home.

Laurel opened the door into a two-room apartment with a small kitchenette. "It's warm in here now, but there's a window air conditioner," she explained. "A senior at the college moved out of the apartment when she graduated last week. It's been thoroughly cleaned since then, so it's ready for occupancy if it suits you."

Micah had noted the rent rate posted on the door, and he said, "Exactly what I need. I've already finished my research on Kentucky's houses and I want to make my headquarters at one location in Tennessee while I travel to the various homes I'm researching. I'll move in now, if that's all right."

"Yes, that's fine with me." She turned on the air conditioner and showed him where extra towels and linens could be found. With her hand on the doorknob, Laurel looked directly into his eyes, the first time she'd had the courage to do so since she'd learned what a terrible mistake she'd made.

"I apologize for my behavior. I've always had a quick temper, and just when I think I have it under control, I act like a shrew. Oaklawn is more than I can handle physically and financially, but my daughter, Debbie, wants to be married here in August. I thought the place should be renovated for that, but the expense has been more than I'd expected. When I worry about my finances, I get irritable. I'm sorry."

Realizing that she was boring this man with her personal problems, she turned away. He'd come to rent an apartment, and she'd not only bawled him out for something that wasn't his fault, but now she was complaining about her financial affairs. She closed the door and left without another word.

Micah had seen the quick rush of tears that glazed Laurel's emerald eyes, and his heart reacted strangely. At first he'd been amused at her caustic comments, but now he felt sorry for her. While he'd been researching other homes, he had met numerous widows who lived in houses that were burdensome, but homes they felt obliged to retain for their children.

While Micah carried his luggage into the apartment, he looked more closely at the large redbrick house, understanding Laurel's frustration. Judging from other homes of this period, he figured the main structure contained eight rooms or more. If he was responsible for a house like Oaklawn, he'd be short-tempered, too.

* * *

Debbie had been away for ten days visiting her fiancé's family in Colorado, but Laurel expected her home for dinner. Conscious of the fact that she'd only have her daughter for a few more months, Laurel prepared some of Debbie's favorite foods for a homecoming dinner.

Laurel had just shaped a pan of rolls and set them aside to rise, when she heard Debbie's voice on the back porch. "Hey, Mom. I'm home. Where are you?"

"In the kitchen."

It had been this way since Debbie had started kindergarten—she always called for her mother as soon as she entered the house. Debbie swept into the kitchen and hugged Laurel. She picked up a carrot from the tray of vegetables Laurel was preparing.

Tears formed in Laurel's eyes, and she looked away to keep Debbie from seeing. She liked Debbie's boyfriend, Dereck, and she wanted them to get married, but it would have been so much easier if he'd gotten a job closer to Oaklawn.

"Missed you, Mom," Debbie said, giving her mother a hug.

"Me, too. How was your trip?" Laurel asked around the knot in her throat.

"Great! Dereck's grandparents live on a ranch, and we spent one day with them. I'd met his parents before, but it was neat to get better acquainted with them. Their home is a lot smaller than ours, and not nearly as old.

Dereck and I looked around for apartments and found one we liked. It's occupied now, but will be free by September. We paid a month's rent for deposit. I took some pictures to show you where I'll be living."

Debbie perched on a high stool and nibbled on the carrot. While she elaborated on the good points of the town that would be her home, Laurel smothered a sigh, already missing her daughter. Debbie's narrow, candid brown eyes mirrored her excitement, and Laurel wondered how she'd ever given birth to a child who was so different from herself.

Debbie had none of Laurel's physical characteristics, and while she didn't look like her father, she bore a marked resemblance to her paternal grandmother, whose youthful portrait hung over the mantel in the parlor. Debbie had a heart-shaped face, with a little nose, uptilted at the end. She wore her light brown hair in a layered bob with a sideswept bang. At five feet nine inches tall, she was a half foot taller than her petite mother. Debbie was even-tempered, a trait she hadn't inherited from either of her parents, for Jason's temper had matched Laurel's own. Perhaps that was one reason they couldn't get along.

"Anything new happening?" Debbie asked, halting Laurel's musings.

"I rented our vacant apartment this afternoon, so that will help pay the bills. I didn't expect to rent it until the fall classes started at the college."

When she recalled her meeting with Micah, Laurel

felt her face flushing, and she was aware that Debbie watched her intently. Her embarrassment was still too keen to talk about her blunder, and Laurel was relieved when Debbie assumed the wrong reason for her mother's heated cheeks.

"Mom, we're spending too much money on the wedding. I can cut back on several things."

"No. You've always dreamed of a big wedding, and you should have what you want. I want the house to look nice for the wedding. Dereck's parents are paying for the rehearsal dinner, and our church family is helping out with food for the reception. We've already paid for your dress, so there shouldn't be a lot more expense. We'll manage."

"What's the new renter like?"

"He has an interesting profession. He's a photojournalist, and he's doing a magazine article on antebellum homes in the area. He wants to feature Oaklawn."

"Awesome! Maybe it's a good thing you fixed up the old place. What's his name?"

"Micah Davidson."

"Oh, I've heard of him! He's world-renowned. His work has been featured on the Discovery Channel and in the *National Geographic*."

A world-renowned journalist and she'd treated him like an errant child! Remembering her faux pas, Laurel wondered what Micah must think of her.

"Will I have time to take my bags upstairs and unpack before supper?" Debbie asked.

"It will be almost an hour before the rolls are ready, so take your time."

While she did a load of laundry and finished supper preparations, Laurel was aware of Micah's movements as he unloaded his car. He left for a short time and came back with two bags from the grocery store. She supposed it would have been a neighborly gesture to invite him to eat with them, although Laurel didn't normally socialize with her renters. But she hadn't had a tenant so near her own age before.

After dinner Debbie went to a party, and since a wispy rainbow indicated a fair evening, Laurel sat on the gallery. The house faced west, and the favorite part of Laurel's day was to sit in a large rocking chair, listening to the birds settling for the night and inhaling the fragrance of the flower gardens, while watching the sun set beyond the distant hills. The scent of roses was especially strong tonight.

Most times when she enjoyed the beauty of her surroundings, Laurel's thoughts were pleasant, but not this evening. It was always this way when she lost her temper. She couldn't remember how many times she'd sat here and asked God's forgiveness for her anger. Every time she thought she'd conquered this weakness, she'd stumble again. She'd lost her temper so many times, it was amazing that she had any left.

God, she silently prayed, *I know Your word teaches to be "slow to become angry," but I did it again today.*

I don't know why You don't lose patience with me, because I'm disobedient so often. But, God, I don't know what the future holds, and I'm afraid. Debbie will be leaving in a few months to live in another state, and I'll be rattling around this old house alone. I have so much to be thankful for, so please forgive me for feeling sorry for myself. Since Jason's parents left the property to me to maintain for Debbie, I feel obligated to stay here. I do love this old place. But sometimes it seems like an albatross around my neck.

As Debbie's wedding date loomed closer, Laurel often experienced her rising fear of being alone. Her daughter had been her whole life for twenty-two years. She didn't want Debbie to suspect her feelings because it would make her sad. But she was determined that Debbie wouldn't realize what a void she was leaving. She would have to develop a new life. She needed to find a job to pay for the renovations, although she knew it would be difficult to venture out on her own after living a sheltered life.

After her husband, Jason, had disappeared in a boating accident, Laurel had dated a few times, but his parents were so opposed to it that she'd given up male companionship rather than live with conflict. Since Jason's body had never been recovered, his parents wouldn't admit that he was really dead, but Laurel had never doubted his death. Jason had been an irresponsible husband, but Laurel didn't believe that he would have deliberately abandoned his family for twenty years. She had never considered remarrying when Debbie was growing up, but now that her daughter was leaving home, perhaps it was time for her to find a companion, someone to date and possibly marry down the line.

Gently, Laurel rocked back and forth, considering her options for a new lifestyle. Micah Davidson walked around the corner of the house with a check in his hand. He came briskly up the steps.

"Good evening, Mrs. Cooper. I'm pleased with the apartment. Here's a month's rent."

Since the man didn't seem to resent her crabby behavior, his presence didn't embarrass Laurel now. She wondered momentarily how old he was. He must be in his late forties, for deep, calipered lines had formed around his generous mouth and streaks of gray frosted his dark hair.

"Won't you sit down?" she invited. "There's going to be a brilliant sunset soon."

Micah took the rocking chair she indicated. "This is a peaceful place. Since you live a mile from the highway, you aren't bothered with the sounds of traffic."

"Sometimes it's *too* peaceful, but I've lived here over half of my life, and I've gotten used to it. I came to Oaklawn as an eighteen-year-old bride, and I haven't been out of Tennessee since my honeymoon."

These weren't pleasant memories, so she said, "Since you're a photojournalist, you must travel a lot and have an interesting life. Tell me about some of your experiences."

"I've spent the past year in the Amazon rain forest with a group of scientists." He grinned in her direction. "That's the reason today's deluge in the backyard didn't bother me. My clothes have been wet most of the time in recent months."

"Mr. Davidson, please," Laurel said, and she feared her face had turned as red as her hair. "I'd like to forget that."

"Sorry," he said contritely, though his face still gleamed with unspoken laughter. "I've written several articles about my experiences in the jungle, and the first one will be published in a few weeks. I'm a free-lance journalist, so I pick and choose what I want to do. I've worked on most of the continents, and, yes, I have had an interesting life. But I'll reach the half-century mark on the last day of June. I can't keep up this pace forever, so it's probably time to establish some roots."

"Don't you have any family?"

"I've never been married, but I have four siblings scattered here and there around the United States. Due to the nature of my work, I don't keep in touch with them, except for an occasional postcard."

"After living such an exciting life for so many years, do you believe you can actually change and be happy with anything else?" She asked this because she was troubled about how to deal with the changes coming soon in her own life.

Micah stood, leaned his tall frame against a column, and looking down at Laurel, he said, "It's possible that

I will be bored with any other life." He shrugged his shoulders. "I really don't know. That's one reason I took this assignment. It's leisurely compared to my usual lifestyle, so it's a good test to determine if I like a slower pace."

"It's usually quiet at Oaklawn, but with Debbie's wedding in August, we'll have more excitement than we normally have." She stood, too. "Would you like to look over the house now?"

"That would be great. I'm studying the architecture as well as the history of the homes, and a preliminary viewing would be helpful."

Chapter Two

They entered the central hall, which boasted a magnificent staircase and a crystal chandelier that had been imported from France in 1835. Laurel explained that this would be the site of Debbie's wedding.

"We can't seat many people in here," she explained, "but since I stood on this stairway during my wedding, just as my mother-in-law did when she was married, Debbie wants to continue the tradition. We'll have only family members for the wedding itself, and then all of our friends and neighbors are invited for the outdoor reception."

The house had four huge rooms on each floor with great fireplaces in each room, set off by carved walnut mantels and varnished paneling. That the Coopers had once been wealthy was evident in the priceless antiques and beautiful oil paintings in each room.

When Micah commented on the wealth of her furnishings, Laurel shrugged her shoulders. "There would be wealth if I sold them, but I want to keep the house as it is for Debbie and her children. This house was one of the few in the area not raided during the Civil War. Most of these furnishings have been here for a long time. Legend has it that the Coopers buried their money and that it was never found. But my father-in-law said his ancestors gave most of their wealth to the war effort. None of the Coopers I know have been prosperous."

In the parlor, Laurel pointed out the Steinway grand piano. "This piano belonged to Debbie's great-grandmother." Laurel ran her fingers over the keys, testing the tone.

"Debbie's father played, and he filled the house with music when he was at home. It's hardly been touched since his death. But Debbie wants her wedding music played on this piano, so I had it tuned."

The house was situated on a small hill, and a spreading lawn with large, gnarled trees and spacious gardens added to the mansion's magnificence. Micah's camera finger was already itching to photograph the place.

Micah thanked Laurel for the tour and returned to his apartment. The rooms were cool now. He turned off the air conditioner and raised the window facing the large stream, flowing southward at the foot of the hill. He inhaled the fragrance of the landscape flowers and settled down with his laptop to map out an itinerary for his Tennessee research.

Micah kept thinking of the delicate bone structure of Laurel's oval face that ended in a determined chin, and he couldn't concentrate on his work. Laurel had experienced a rough life bringing up her child as a single parent, but she'd apparently developed a strong character, while fulfilling her role as a mother. He remembered how her emerald eyes easily flared with anger as bright as a flash of lightning, only to fade just as quickly to the softness of a peaceful ocean. Her auburn hair was cut close to her head like a cap. Since she'd been dressed in jeans, he was well aware of her slim waist above shapely hips, and—

"Whoa!" Micah said aloud.

He shook his head, wondering at his thoughts. It had been a long time since he'd given *any* thought to a woman. There was no time for romance in his busy schedule, so what had prompted this sudden surge of interest in Laurel Cooper? He decided he was just as well off not to know the answer to that one, and he shifted his thoughts to the computer screen.

By the time they'd finished their tour of the house, Laurel had been completely at ease with Micah, and now she could smile at the way she'd mistaken him for a carpenter. She thought about his interesting life— how much he'd seen of the world compared to her meager travels.

She had eventually become resigned to her restricted life. Since Debbie was all they had left of their son, the

Coopers were determined that their granddaughter would be raised in their home. When Laurel had mentioned going to work, or moving into a home of her own, they'd raised such a fuss that it was easier to submit to their demands rather than fight them.

She'd tried to stifle her temper when dealing with them, because they'd aged considerably after Jason was lost at sea. They'd been good to her in many ways, but she hadn't had a life of her own. She'd received some income from a small trust fund left by her grandmother, but she was dependent on them for food and housing. And she could never have given Debbie a good education without their help.

She was surprised when they'd left everything to her, although her father-in-law had asked her in his will to keep Oaklawn for Debbie's inheritance, actually controlling her life after his death. Mrs. Cooper had lived only two months after her husband, and by the time Laurel had paid their funeral expenses, there wasn't much money left.

Acting on the advice of her attorney, Kevin Cooper, Laurel had used most of that money to redo the wing into apartments. Kevin, a first cousin of Jason's, had advised that the apartments would provide a steady income for her. The apartments had supplied an income, but by the time she paid the utilities and the taxes, she'd hardly broken even on the apartments. Laurel still had the upkeep of a large house, a limited income and no job experience. She was annoyed that Kevin had given her such poor advice, but she hadn't complained to him. He'd been helpful in settling her father-in-law's estate, and he'd assured her that she could call on him for further help when needed.

Although she'd been concerned about having Debbie leave home, Laurel wondered if it wouldn't be nice to be completely independent for a change. At forty-two she could still get an education and have a career. She had been dreading the summer, but she anticipated it now. She intended to enjoy her daughter's company while they planned the wedding. And since just one evening in Micah's company had uplifted her spirits, she looked forward to seeing him often during the next few weeks.

It was amazing how quickly she'd been drawn to Micah. She hadn't dated much before she'd met and married Jason, and since his death she hadn't been interested enough in any man to contemplate a serious relationship with him. But Micah's quiet ways, his dry humor and his gentleness had captivated her from the first.

Laurel was still downstairs when she noticed the lights go off in Micah's apartment. The clock on the stairway chimed ten, and Laurel knew it wouldn't be long until Debbie came home. She turned off all of the downstairs lights except the ones on the back porch and in the entry hall and went upstairs. She always stayed awake until she knew Debbie was safe at home, but Laurel had avoided being a controlling mother who monitored her daughter's comings and goings. If Debbie wanted to talk to her about what she'd done when she was out for an evening, Laurel let her take the initiative.

After her in-laws died, Laurel had moved into their room because it commanded a good view of the river valley. She had kept the cherry bed, dresser and chest that had been handed down for several generations. But to give the room a hint of her own personality, she'd had a green carpet laid and dressed the high, narrow windows in ruffled curtains that matched the rug's color. As a final touch, she'd replaced the dark painted walls with a colorful, floral wallpaper.

Laurel had changed into a mint-green cotton nightgown by the time she heard Debbie's light gait, taking the steps, two at a time. The door cracked slightly and Debbie whispered, "Asleep, Mom?"

"No, come in. I'm about ready for bed."

"We had a fun time at the pastor's house, but I almost went to sleep two or three times. It was a long flight from Colorado today." Debbie smothered a yawn and drifted over to kiss Laurel's cheek. "Night, Mom."

"We should go into Knoxville and pick up your wedding invitations tomorrow," Laurel said, "but we won't have to leave early. Sleep late if you want to."

Yawning again, Debbie waved lazily, indicating she'd understood and wandered out of the room and down the hall.

Laurel sat in the wicker rocker she'd brought from

her grandmother's home and reached for the Bible on the small table beside the bed. For the past year, Laurel had memorized a different Scripture verse each week and used it for her special meditation. Without opening the Bible, she tried to remember this week's verse from the book of Proverbs. *A cheerful heart is good medicine.*

Despite her difficult life, Laurel had, for the most part, remained cheerful. She and Jason had enjoyed a happy marriage for eighteen months until Debbie was born. But Jason had wanted Laurel's full attention, and he resented Debbie's claims on her. Although Debbie had toddled after him all the time, he hadn't had time for her. He worked on construction jobs that took him away for months at a time. He kept in touch with his family with occasional phone calls and infrequent checks to Laurel. Jason's parents had spoiled him as a child, and he hadn't grown up to be a responsible adult. While he was working in Texas, he'd met Ryan Bledsoe, and for a year prior to his death, Jason had bummed around the country with his friend.

During those difficult days, and the time after Jason's death, Laurel had relied on her faith in God to survive. He hadn't failed her. She'd prayed for the wisdom and strength to be a good mother, and God had answered her prayer. He'd given her the strength to keep her in-laws from spoiling their granddaughter as they had their son.

Debbie had never caused her any trouble. In high school, she'd made good grades, played in the band

and participated in summer sports. Despite the sorrow that Laurel personally felt, she had kept her sadness from Debbie. And because of her upbeat attitude, Laurel had kept her head above water when circumstances tended to overwhelm her.

Laurel opened the double windows facing the bend in the river. The cost of air-conditioning this huge house was prohibitive, so during the summer, they stored cool air at nighttime and kept the windows and doors closed all day. The thick brick walls retained the cool air that drifted inside at night.

Before she turned off the light, Laurel walked across the hall and into the dark room she'd once shared with Jason. She pulled back the heavy draperies and opened the window, providing a full view of the addition where the apartments were located.

She wondered if Micah found it difficult to sleep in strange surroundings. Probably not, since he'd traveled so much. What would it be like to travel as extensively as he had? Her honeymoon to Atlanta was the farthest she'd been away from Oaklawn. Dereck's mother had invited her to come visit them, but with her renovation debts, Laurel was short of funds. She'd have to be conservative until she took a job and paid off that loan. Perhaps then she could go to visit Debbie and Dereck in Colorado.

Laurel hummed a hymn as she darkened her room and turned on a dim light beside her bed. She stretched, savoring the texture of the smooth sheets under her back. She crossed her hands behind her neck and listened to the cacophony of insect sounds outside the window. She also heard a cow bawling on her neighbor's farm—probably trying to find its calf. The owl, nesting in the attic of Oaklawn's garden house, serenaded its nesting mate. Last night the plaintive call of the owl had made her sad, but tonight she enjoyed it.

Micah's coming had lifted her spirits. The rent he paid this summer would help with her finances, but she wasn't sure that was the only reason she was pleased with her new tenant. She fell asleep thinking about him.

The ringing phone woke Laurel, and at first she thought it was the alarm clock, which she'd set for seven. A glance at the clock indicated it was after midnight. Her heart thumped rapidly, and her stomach churned with anxiety and apprehension. Following her in-laws' custom, Laurel had developed the habit of going to bed early. Her friends knew she didn't keep late hours, so who could be calling? She sat up and quickly lifted the receiver, hoping the phone hadn't wakened Debbie. Maybe there was an emergency among the church family.

She swallowed with difficulty and hesitantly answered. "Hello?"

Her apprehension increased when no one answered her greeting. She knew someone was on the line because she heard uneven breathing. She almost dropped the phone when a pleasant, tenor voice started singing the words of an old song.

"I looked over Jordan, and what did I see
Coming for to carry me home?
A band of angels coming after me,
Coming for to carry me home."

After a significant pause, the man said, "Be ready, Laurel, we're coming after you."

Laurel dropped the phone receiver on the floor, and reached out a trembling finger to sever the connection. She childishly pinched her arm to be sure she wasn't dreaming.

She ran to the bathroom, sick to her stomach, and retched. Laurel rinsed her mouth, gulped a glass of water and staggered back to bed.

She was sorry now that she hadn't stayed on the phone. She replaced the phone in its cradle and lay awake the rest of the night. Was there any way she could trace the call?

After she'd squirmed in the bed for several hours, Laurel got up, dressed in an ankle-length floral skirt and a soft, white cotton blouse, and quietly went downstairs. Because of the isolation of the house, she had two dusk-to-dawn security lights, which kept the grounds and the house partially illuminated all night long. Creeping along in the muted light, Laurel entered the kitchen and closed the door so she wouldn't wake Debbie. She filled the teakettle with water and, while she waited for it to boil, placed a tea bag in her favorite mug.

Once made, Laurel wrapped her hands around the steaming cup and went to the screened back porch, where she'd encountered Micah yesterday. The front gallery contained only antique rocking chairs, but after she'd taken over ownership of the house, Laurel had made the back porch into a cozy, relaxing area.

Laurel sat on a padded lounge chair and sipped the tea as she contemplated what to do. If she'd had caller ID, she might have determined the identity of her caller, but with her limited income, she cut corners when she could, and the latest technology wasn't high on her priority list.

When daylight dispelled the darkness, Laurel became aware of movement at her side. Remembering the threatening phone call, the cup tottered in her hand. Micah Davidson walked across the lawn. He halted when he saw her, and momentarily she wondered if he'd been the caller.

"Good morning," he said. "You're up early."

"Earlier than usual," she answered. "Couldn't you sleep?"

"I don't usually sleep more than six hours, and I went to bed early. I had breakfast while I waited for enough daylight to look around. You don't mind if I explore your property, do you?"

"Of course not. There's a cleared path to the river if you want to go that way."

"That's where I was heading. Would you have time to walk with me? I could use a guide."

"Yes, I'd like a walk," she said eagerly. She wasn't in the mood for conversation, but it might be a good idea to learn more about Micah Davidson. She swung her feet off the lounge, kicked off the soft scuffs she wore and reached under the chair for a pair of walking shoes. She quickly pulled on the socks she'd stored in the toes of the shoes, and in a few minutes had joined Micah.

Pointing to the left, Laurel said, "The best path is through the orchard."

The lawn was neatly mowed until they reached the orchard, then weeds grew profusely in the path. Laurel's long skirt was soon wet from the abundant dew on the grass.

"In your research of Southern homes, you've probably heard many stories about keepsakes the Confederates buried before the invaders came. I mentioned Oaklawn's story to you last night. Supposedly a Cooper ancestor buried gold and silver in this orchard, but the cache was never found."

"Not even after the war?"

"No," Laurel said, and her eyes sparkled, temporarily replacing the pain Micah had noticed. "My father-in-law said that when he was a boy, he and his brother dug from one end of that field to the other and didn't find any money. But the cultivation did give them a bumper crop of fruit for a few years."

Micah gazed appreciatively at the grainfields and the lush pastureland along the river.

"Oaklawn isn't as large as it was in the eighteenth

century," Laurel continued as they walked. "At one time, the Coopers owned a thousand acres, but they've had to sell parcels of land during hard times. The farm is only fifty acres now. Actually, I'm glad it's no more than that, because I can't even manage that much land. My neighbor, Pete Howe, rents the farmland, so I only care for the few acres around the house. I have a riding mower, so it isn't difficult work, but it does keep me busy during the summer. Especially this year, when I want everything to look nice for the wedding."

Although she'd hoped walking would take her mind off the mysterious phone call, it didn't, and she lapsed into silence, trying to figure out who had called her. The singer's voice didn't sound familiar at all.

Micah walked slightly behind Laurel since the path was narrow, but he was aware of her downcast eyes. When she'd joined him for the walk, he'd noticed at once that she wasn't the contented woman he'd talked with on the gallery the night before. Had something happened to disturb her, or did it take a while for her to get going in the morning?

"I'd appreciate hearing anything you know about Oaklawn," Micah said. "I want to feature the history of the homes, as well as the architecture."

Laurel wasn't in the mood for visiting, but taking a deep breath and staring straight ahead as they walked, she said, "The Coopers moved here soon after the Revolutionary War. The place was a wilderness then. They lived in log cabins and had the usual troubles with the

Native Americans that most settlers had. Eventually they prospered enough for Debbie's great-great-grandfather to build the original brick house, but the Cooper wealth declined over the next century."

When they passed a knoll where the family cemetery was located, Micah commented, "I suppose your husband is buried here."

"No, he isn't," she said bluntly, because she didn't like to think about Jason's death.

Micah couldn't imagine why his question had annoyed her. They were both silent as they walked downhill to the northern bank of the shallow river. A wide beach of sand and gravel had formed at a sharp bend in the stream. Overhanging trees provided a secluded area. A few ramshackle lawn chairs and a wooden bench had been placed several feet from the water. Laurel walked to one of the sturdier chairs and sat down.

"Do people go swimming or fishing here?"

"Mostly fishing," Laurel said shortly, her eyes on the river.

Did his presence annoy her, or was she troubled about something else?

After a pause, she continued, "But there is a deep pool midway in the stream. The local boys go to the other side of the river, swing on the vines and drop into the pool. It's a dangerous practice. One boy was seriously hurt here last summer, but they continue to swim."

The gentle ripple of the water as it slid past them was quieting, and the peace of the place was soothing to

Micah. After spending over a year in the jungle, the past three months in the States—mostly in cities—had frustrated him. The noise of traffic had grated on his nerves. Pleased to have this sojourn in a quiet place, Micah sat on the wooden bench facing upstream. In this position, he could watch Laurel without being obvious about it.

Her present attitude didn't compare to her quick flash of anger yesterday, which had disappeared as quickly as it had come. Her eyes brooded today, and there was a petulant droop to her full lips.

Early sunlight peeked into the shaded glade, a fish flipped in the middle of the stream and birds gently began their morning songs.

Without looking at him, her eyes staring across the river, Laurel said, "Mr. Davidson, I should apologize to you again. I had an unpleasant experience last night, or I wouldn't have been so short-tempered. Let me give you a reasonable answer to your question about my husband's burial. It's always been a sore subject to me, but you wouldn't have known that."

Chapter Three

Several minutes passed before Laurel continued, and to spare her embarrassment, Micah kept his eyes on the river. A small flock of ducks drifted lazily with the current. Occasionally, one of them would tilt forward into the river for a morning snack.

"Twenty years ago, Jason and a friend were sailing off the Atlantic coast of South America, and their boat capsized," Laurel said quietly. "Their bodies were never recovered. He was an only child, and his parents never got over his death."

He noticed that she didn't mention her own sorrow. If she'd been a widow for so long, perhaps the pain was gone. But why hadn't she remarried? Judging by his own immediate attraction to her, she must have had plenty of suitors.

As though she read his thoughts, Laurel said, "Debbie, who was only two at the time, was all his parents had left of Jason. As I mentioned last night, they insisted that I stay at Oaklawn and raise my child here. I was glad to stay, because I didn't have any other place to go."

Many questions rose in Micah's mind. Why was her husband's death a sore point? She spoke as if she resented him, but it wasn't any of his business. Laurel would tell him what she wanted him to know.

"Although it's been a labor of love to rear Debbie as a single parent, it hasn't been easy for me. I'm ashamed to admit it, but I've always resented Jason taking that trip and getting killed when he should have stayed home and looked after his family. Debbie has missed a lot by not having a father."

Micah silently thought that Debbie might have been better off without her father's presence. Jason Cooper sounded like a selfish man.

"His parents hoped almost to the end that Jason was still alive. When they at last conceded that he was dead, they didn't live long. My mother-in-law survived her husband by two months. They wanted me to preserve the house for Debbie. I'm trying to do what they asked me to."

"It hasn't been easy for you, I'm sure."

She nodded sadly. "Besides the work, it's a financial burden. As soon as Debbie is married, I intend to find a job, even though I have no marketable work skills. She'll be moving to Colorado, so I'll have lots of time on my hands. I've been looking into possible employment, but I don't have many job skills. I'm considering taking a two-year business course at the college. But these decisions are on hold until Debbie is married."

She stood up quickly. "And speaking of Debbie, we're going into Knoxville this morning, so I have to go back to the house."

"I have an appointment to look over a home in Nashville today, so I want to get started, too."

They didn't talk as they returned to the house, but Micah hummed in a monotone that grated on Laurel's already distraught nerves. She tried to determine the tune, but if he had any particular song in mind, it was one she didn't know.

"Thanks for walking with me. I like to be outdoors early in the morning," he said, giving her a sideways glance.

"So do I. Take care while you're traveling today," she answered, and he favored her with a wide smile.

"Mom, what is wrong with you?" Debbie asked in the midst of a disastrous breakfast. Laurel had burned the grits, upended a cup of coffee on the tablecloth and, instead of providing jelly for their toast, picked up a jar of mustard and slid it across the table. "I've never seen you so jumpy. Are you sick?"

Sitting down and gripping her hands in her lap underneath the table, Laurel tried to calm her inner trembling.

"I didn't sleep much last night," she said, unable to

stifle the tremor in her voice. "I'll be all right as soon as I've had a cup of coffee."

To prove her point, Laurel poured another cup. Coffee sloshed over the brim and into the saucer as she lifted the cup. Debbie cast another startled glance toward her.

"Go back to bed, and forget the trip to Knoxville," Debbie said, concern in her voice. "We can pick up the invitations tomorrow."

"Oh, no," Laurel said, and forced a smile. "I want to go today." She had to do something to keep her mind off of her nighttime caller.

Sensing Debbie's gaze upon her again, Laurel knew she was staring fixedly out the window. Determined to retain some sense of normalcy, she spread butter over the grits on her plate and ate them and the egg in front of her as if she had a good appetite.

"If you want to fill the dishwasher, I'll go upstairs and get ready."

"I'll take care of everything, but I still think we should postpone our trip," Debbie insisted.

Laurel forced a laugh. "This isn't the first time I've been tired when I've gotten out of bcd. Let's plan to leave in an hour."

While she luxuriated in the big bathtub and lathered vigorously with her lavender-scented bath gel, Laurel thought about Micah Davidson. Although she'd fleetingly wondered if Micah could have been the midnight caller, after she'd heard him humming this morning, she'd discounted that idea. Micah had a bass voice, and he couldn't carry a tune. The man on the phone had a melodious tenor voice. Thinking about Micah lifted Laurel's spirits, and she decided she wouldn't allow last night's incident to ruin her day with Debbie.

Stepping from the tub, Laurel patted her body dry with a large towel. She applied body lotion, and for a moment her worries receded as the lotion soothed her body. Laurel habitually denied herself for others, but she did indulge herself with a fragrant bath.

After dressing in a pair of striped capris and a white knit blouse, she sat in her grandmother's rocking chair for her morning devotions. She felt close to her grandmother in this chair, since she was the one who had guided Laurel's spiritual maturation. She turned to her grandmother's favorite Scripture in the book of Philippians and read softly.

"'I have learned the secret of being content in any and every situation, whether well fed or hungry, whether living in plenty or in want. I can do everything through Him who gives me strength.'"

Her grandmother hadn't had an easy life, but she'd never doubted that God had sustained her through each problem. Laurel, too, had experienced enough sorrow since her marriage to make her bitter, but she'd kept a degree of contentment, in spite of the circumstances.

Fortified by the words she'd read, Laurel left her room with less trepidation than she'd had since that mysterious phone call. As soon as she and Debbie drove away from Oaklawn, Laurel pushed the call to the back of her mind. They had a pleasant day as they picked up the wedding invitations, registered for more of Debbie's gift preferences at two stores and enjoyed a lunch in their favorite Chinese restaurant.

For the next two nights, knowing that she was taking the coward's way out, Laurel disconnected the phone when she went to bed. Although her body tensed each time she heard the phone during the day, she had no mysterious messages. Occasionally, she wondered if the call had been a dream.

Debbie worked on the evening shift at a fast-food restaurant in Knoxville. For the first three days after he'd moved into the apartment, Micah also left early and didn't return until late, so Laurel was alone most of the time. On Saturday evening, as Laurel sat on the gallery, she heard a car approaching. When she saw that it was Micah, she waved to him. In a short time, she heard his steps on the graveled pathway.

"Good evening, Mrs. Cooper," he said.

"You might as well call me Laurel. We're not very formal in this neighborhood."

"I'm not formal at all," he said, "So good evening, Laurel."

A dimple at the corner of her mouth deepened. "Hello, Micah. You're home early."

"Yes. I've had a busy week, so I'm ready for some rest."

"Come and sit down," she invited. "This is a good place to relax. It's been a hectic week for me, too, and I had to take time to let my body catch up with my soul. I'm preparing myself for worship tomorrow. Will you go to church with us in the morning?"

Settling down in the rocking chair beside her and stretching out his long legs, Micah said, "I haven't been to church for so long, I wouldn't know how to act."

With a smile, Laurel said, "I doubt things have changed much since you used to go to church. We have a small sanctuary and a simple order of worship. You wouldn't have a problem."

"Fact is," Micah said, "I'm not much interested in organized churches anymore. I've spent my adult life traveling, mostly in isolated places, where there aren't any church buildings. I worship the God of Creation. I can have 'church' anywhere."

Disturbed by his comments, Laurel said, "I'm sure that's true, but don't you miss the fellowship of other Christians? I need the strength and support I receive on Sunday to deal with any problems I might have during the week."

Micah seemed to deliberate a few moments before he answered. "In my line of work, sometimes months pass without the opportunity to worship with a congregation. But when I see God's handiwork in what He's created—the skies, the trees, the animals—it's easy for me to worship."

Laurel wasn't normally argumentative about the

Scriptures, but she had the feeling that Micah was missing the most important principle. "That's all well and good," she said, "as long as you acknowledge the place of Jesus, God's Son, in the creation of the world."

Micah looked puzzled, and he said, "I remember something about that from my childhood when I went to Sunday School."

Laurel didn't press her opinion at that time. She, too, could see God in the universe around her. And she believed it was only a short distance from acknowledging God, Who created the world, and believing that His Son, Jesus, was the Savior of mankind. She doubted that Micah had made that connection.

"Then you will go to church with Debbie and me tomorrow?"

"Yes, thank you. I'm looking forward to meeting your daughter. With my long hours, I've missed my chances so far."

Laurel said proudly, "I know I'm prejudiced, but she *is* a fine girl."

Micah thought if Debbie was anything like her mother, she would be worth meeting.

Hesitantly, Laurel continued, "If we're asking something that you don't want to do, please say so. But Debbie wants to know if you'll consider photographing her wedding on August twenty-fifth. Will you still be in Tennessee then?"

"I'm not sure, but if I agree to photograph the wedding, I'll come back for it. But you should know that, although I've photographed a few weddings, I'm not at my best when photographing people. I prefer landscapes or anything in the natural environment."

"Let me show you what we have in mind before you make a commitment."

A gentle breeze blew from the river as they walked into the wide expanse of yard to the left of the house. The breeze ruffled Laurel's red curls, and as she pointed out various things, Micah observed her, wondering that her red hair hadn't a trace of gray. Modern hair colors could work wonders, but he doubted there was a rinse on her hair.

"We've chosen the southern lawn for the reception," she explained. "We're planning an early afternoon wedding, and the house will shade most of this area. The lawn is rather spacious, as you can see. We're expecting about a hundred guests, but it's an open wedding list, so it's difficult to know how many we'll have. We've rented tents and tables. If we have an overflow, some of them can sit under the shade trees. The ladies of our church are cooking the dinner."

Micah sauntered around the area, looking at it with his professional eye, considering the shading and judging the position of the sun in three months.

"What time is the ceremony?" he asked.

"The music will start at one o'clock, and the processional a half hour later."

"Then, I'd say this is an ideal spot. The light should be good for photographs."

"The formal pictures will be taken inside. We want candid shots of activities here on the lawn. Dereck's father plans to make a video, but we want some professional pictures for albums."

"Are they having many attendants?"

"Just one each, plus a flower girl and a ring bearer— Dereck's niece and nephew." She halted, and looked out over the river. "Without any close male relatives, I'll have to give her away."

Her voice faltered a little, and Micah quickly glanced her way. "Pretty difficult to do, huh?" he said sympathetically.

"Yes, especially since they're moving to Colorado. The groom is an engineer, and he has a job there. Besides, Colorado is his home state."

"And you'll be all alone."

Laurel turned away and started walking toward the house.

"I'm sorry, Laurel. I shouldn't have said that. Not being a parent, I can't quite understand your fears."

"You don't need to apologize. I will miss her, but I've tried not to tie her to my apron strings. I've learned to love Oaklawn, but in a way, it's been a prison to me. I'm trying to preserve the place for Debbie, never knowing if she'll ever want to live here. Her future husband travels a lot with his job, but I don't want her to feel tied to Oaklawn. I'm anticipating Debbie's wedding as a turning point in my life, too."

He followed her up the steps to the gallery.

"I'll be happy to photograph the wedding."

"Thank you so much," Laurel said. "Debbie will be very pleased."

Laurel felt a welcome surge of excitement. She was assured of Micah's presence the rest of the summer, and she could have shouted for joy. Trying to control her exuberance, she said, "We'll start for church at ten-thirty."

Micah said good-night and sauntered toward his apartment. But he turned back, and at his quiet approach, he saw that Laurel sat with her head in her hands. He scuffled his feet, and when he reached the steps of the gallery, she was sitting erect, her eyes suspiciously moist.

"Will you and Debbie go with me for lunch after church?"

"That's nice of you," she said. "I don't know Debbie's work schedule for Sunday, but she tries not to work on Sunday morning. Thanks for asking us."

"Since I'm new in the area, I'll leave it up to you to choose a restaurant."

Laurel nodded, but the despair in her eyes saddened him. She was disturbed about something, and he didn't think it was Debbie's leaving. Micah wanted to help, but he couldn't intrude into a place Laurel didn't want him to go.

Chapter Four

Micah would never have dreamed that Sunday morning would find him searching the closet to find something suitable to wear to church. Why had he accepted Laurel's invitation to go with her today, when he hadn't attended an organized worship service for years?

He hadn't thought he'd need dress clothes for the summer, and most of his garments consisted of denim pants and shorts. His suits and ties were at his house in Kansas. He sorted through his garment bags and came up with a new polo shirt and a pair of trousers, both in need of pressing. Laurel had provided an ironing board and iron for her renters, and while he waited for the iron to heat, Micah shined his shoes.

He hoped his casual clothes would be acceptable at Laurel's church. Not that he ever gave much thought to what people thought, but he didn't want Laurel to be ashamed of his appearance. Confused by his preoccupation with Laurel and her affairs, he wandered restlessly around the apartment.

He couldn't understand her obvious attachment to Oaklawn. He'd been on the move all of his adult life, and the only land he owned was a quarter-section of farmland in Kansas. He'd inherited the property from a maternal uncle a few years ago, and he used the farm to store the possessions he couldn't haul around with him.

He rented the land to a farmer whose farm adjoined his, and the farmer's wife cleaned and aired his four-room house monthly. The farm was valuable to him as a good source of income, but he visited the place infrequently. Obviously, Laurel wasn't making much money from Oaklawn, so her attachment to the place must be sentimental.

As Micah paced, he wondered why he couldn't put down roots like other people. Was he destined to be a wanderer to the end of his days? He didn't want to settle down in Kansas, which was hot and dry in summer and cold and windy in the winter. Micah felt as strong and competent as he had when he was a teenager. He had several years before he needed to retire, so why was he thinking of settling down? Not willing to acknowledge the reason for his discontent, he decided to put these perplexing emotions out of his mind.

When he finished dressing and took a look in the full-length mirror on the closet door, Micah decided he looked acceptable. Laurel had said the church was small, and it was a hot morning, so he assumed none of the men would be wearing suits.

After he cleared the seats of the car and put all of his photographic equipment in the apartment, he tapped on Laurel's back door. A lovely sight in her Sunday-go-to-meeting clothes, Laurel opened the door and greeted him. He thought she looked like a child playacting in her mother's clothes. With her diminutive stature, delicate body, and a shy smile hovering on her lips, she seemed like a little girl dressed up for her first party. She wore an ankle-length black skirt and black sandals. The scoop-necked blouse was an ivory color that blended charmingly with her pearl-like complexion.

When Laurel's lashes dropped, and a telltale flush appeared on her cheeks, Micah realized he'd been staring.

"Good morning, Laurel," he said. "Am I too early?"

"Not at all," she stammered, still flustered by Micah's intent appraisal. "Debbie is a little late. We both overslept this morning."

She motioned to the chairs on the porch. "Shall we sit and wait for her? We still have half an hour before services begin, and it's only a ten-minute drive to Bethel Church."

But before they could be seated, quick steps sounded in the hallway, and Debbie stepped out on the porch. She was a pretty young woman of above average height, but she had few characteristics of her petite mother. Debbie's hair was straight instead of curly. Her eyes were brown instead of green. Apparently Debbie looked like her father's side of the family. Since Debbie was dressed in casual slacks and a knit blouse, Micah decided that his attire was suitable for their church.

"Have I kept you waiting long?" she asked.

"Debbie," Laurel said, "this is Micah Davidson." And looking at her daughter with unmistakable pride, she added, "Micah, my daughter, Debbie."

"Pleased to meet you, Mr. Davidson," Debbie said with genuine warmth. "I've seen your work featured on TV several times. You're a fantastic photographer."

"Thanks. I enjoy my work."

"Have you ever considered writing a book about your exploits?"

"I'm having one published in a few months," he said, with a wide smile.

Out of the corner of his eye, Micah noticed that Laurel was fidgeting from one foot to the other.

"Should we go now?" he asked.

"Yes," Laurel said. "I don't want to be late. You sit in the front seat, Debbie, you're better at giving directions than I am."

They passed Walden College on the way to worship, and Micah wondered why he was hesitant to tell Laurel he'd been invited to teach there.

The sedate brick buildings, dating to the early twentieth century, looked quiet and confining. After he'd been his own taskmaster for twenty-five years, could he endure working on a regular, day-by-day schedule arranged by someone else? Was he too set in his ways to ever change?

He turned his thoughts from the college to another unaccustomed experience when Debbie, who sat beside him on the front seat, directed him to the parking lot of Bethel Church. According to the sign over the door, the church had been built in 1910. When Micah followed Debbie and Laurel up the center aisle into the small sanctuary, he admired the Gothic-style architecture of the windows and the ceiling, as well as the ornately carved pews. They sat beside a stained-glass window placed in memory of the Cooper family.

The soft strains of the organ music were peaceful, but Micah momentarily longed for the soft stirring of the wind and the sounds of nature that he usually heard when he worshiped. Sitting between Debbie and Laurel, he felt confined like a bird with its wings clipped, as if his spirit could never soar again.

He probably would have bolted if he'd had free access to the door, but when an usher raised all the windows in the sanctuary, he could hear birds singing. A gentle breeze wafted the strong scent of honeysuckle into the church. He breathed deeply of the fresh air and relaxed.

Micah took a quick survey of the congregation, seeing only one man, other than the minister, who had on a suit and tie.

Laurel handed Micah a hymnal when the preacher announced the first song. It was a song he didn't know, but he followed the words on the page as he listened to Debbie's strong soprano blending with Laurel's alto voice. Micah had been told by a high-school music teacher that he had a pleasant speaking voice, but when he sang, he croaked like a frog. Thereafter, he'd never joined in group singing, but when he was out on a job alone, he'd belt out the words of any song that took his fancy, with or without a tune. A croaking frog was acceptable in the great outdoors.

When the pastor asked for unspoken requests before the morning prayer, Laurel lifted her hand. The haunted expression Micah had seen in her eyes when they'd walked yesterday morning had returned. And during the prayer, he sensed her lips were moving in silent petition.

Micah had a Bible somewhere among his possessions, but he hadn't carried it on his travels, and he hadn't read it for a long time. His parents had instilled a belief in God in his heart, but even as a child he'd avoided group worship. Everything he photographed, especially the different species of animals and plants he'd seen in various parts of the world, had filled him with wonder and awe at the majesty of the God Who had created the world.

Bruce Jensen, the preacher, was an unpretentious, thin, middle-aged man, but he was sincere and his obvious knowledge held Micah's attention. He listened eagerly as Pastor Jensen started his sermon.

According to the preacher, Jesus and His disciples had been traveling through Samaria when they'd encountered a woman with a bad reputation. She had attempted to conceal her lifestyle by comparing the Jewish method of worship with the way the Samaritans worshiped.

Intrigued by this subject that was of importance to him, Micah listened intently when Pastor Jensen read a few verses from the Bible, giving the reference as the fourth chapter of John.

"A time is coming and has now come when the true worshipers will worship the Father in spirit and truth, for they are the kind of worshipers the Father seeks. God is a spirit, and His worshipers must worship in spirit and in truth."

According to these words, his method of worship was as valid as the way Laurel worshiped. But doubt arose in Micah's heart as the preacher explained the passage more fully. In summing up the conversation between Jesus and the Samaritan Woman, Pastor Jensen said that Jesus turned the subject from the *place* where one worships to the *Person* who is worshiped. He explained that God is the Lord of all, and that He *can* be worshiped anywhere. But the only acceptable worship involves the entire heart, mind and the truth of God as revealed in the Scripture.

To that point, the preacher's message and Micah's method of worship seemed compatible. But when Pastor Jensen continued, Micah conceded that he may have missed the essence of true worship.

"When people asked Jesus to show them the way to God, He had replied, 'I and the Father are one. He who has seen me has seen the Father.' At a later time, Jesus had said, 'No man cometh to the Father except by me.'"

Pastor Jensen concluded his message by quoting another Scripture, "'He who does not honor the Son does not honor the Father who sent Him.' Until people accept Jesus, the Son of God, into their hearts, there can be no worship."

As the congregation rose for the benediction, Micah realized that if the preacher's words were true, his methods of worship had not pleased God.

Micah had his hand wrung by most of the congregation at the end of the service, and he had many invitations to become a part of their fellowship while he was in the community. While Laurel and Debbie visited with their friends, he circled the building looking with interest at the architecture. If he accepted a position at Walden College, he might research historic churches of the South for an article or a TV feature. Bethel Church could be included.

"Where are we going for lunch?" he asked as he opened the car doors. Again, Laurel took the back seat, leaving the front for Debbie.

"You call it, Mom. Where do you want to go?"

"How about that nice Sunday buffet at the restaurant on the road to Knoxville? They have a good choice of food."

"Give me directions, Debbie," Micah said.

As he started the engine, she said, "Oh, wait. Here comes our cousin, Kevin. He must want to meet you."

But the man approached the passenger side of the car. He opened the rear door and handed an envelope to Laurel.

"I was worried I'd miss you today. This letter came to my office last week. I've intended to drop by Oaklawn and give it to you, but I've been busy."

Laurel took the envelope and glanced at the typed address. "Mrs. Jason Cooper, c/o Kevin Cooper, Attorney at Law." She hadn't had a letter addressed to Mrs. Jason Cooper for a long time. Her hands stiffened and her eyes blurred. Could this have anything to do with her mysterious phone call?

She was thankful for a moment to compose herself when Debbie said, "Cousin Kevin, did you meet our tenant? Kevin Cooper, Micah Davidson," she said.

Kevin Cooper extended a hand across the front seat and gave Micah a hearty handshake. Kevin was the only man other than the minister who'd been wearing a suit. He was a tall, portly man with a mane of shoulder-length gray hair and a full gray beard. His appearance reminded Micah of an antebellum Southern planter.

"Going to stay long at Oaklawn?" Kevin said.

"Two or three months," Micah answered.

"Everything going all right, Laurel?" Kevin asked affably.

"Yes, the wedding plans are moving along quite well," she said with an effort.

"Glad to hear it," her cousin-in-law said. "I'll try to

stop by this week. Glad to meet you, Mr. Davidson. It relieves my mind that you'll be around Oaklawn this summer. When the apartments are empty, I worry about my cousins living in such an isolated place."

Kevin closed the door and Micah drove out of the church parking lot.

"Cousin Kevin is a nice guy," Debbie said. "He was my daddy's second cousin, and he's been very good to Mom and me after my grandparents died. If he's worried about the *two* of us living alone at Oaklawn, I don't know what he'll think when Mom is there by herself."

Laurel remained silent.

Following Debbie's instructions, Micah left the narrow county road and accessed the highway. Micah had been prepared to dislike Debbie, because he'd gotten the impression that she imposed on her mother. Or at least he'd gathered that Laurel carried the whole burden of family decisions. After chatting with her about college life and her upcoming marriage, he decided she wasn't a spoiled brat, but an intelligent, compassionate young lady.

Suddenly it occurred to Micah that Laurel hadn't said a word since they'd left the churchyard, and he glanced quickly over his shoulder. Her eyes were closed, her face was the color of ashes, and her hand crushed the letter Kevin Cooper had given her.

"Hey, Mom," Debbie said, not looking at her mother, but indicating a turn that Micah should take. "Who was your letter from?"

Micah heard Laurel open and close her purse. As he

made the sharp left-hand turn, he had a slight glimpse of Laurel's hands. The letter wasn't in sight.

"Oh, just a piece of junk mail."

"Seems strange anyone would send your mail to Cousin Kevin's office."

Laurel didn't answer.

"Probably one of your admirers sneaking a letter to you so I wouldn't see it," Debbie teased.

If she had been disturbed by the letter's contents, Laurel had regained her composure by the time they reached the restaurant. But her gaiety seemed forced, and occasionally her eyes held a resentful, frightened look. Debbie didn't seem to notice, so Micah wondered if he was imagining things. Maybe the letter *had* been junk mail, but he didn't think so.

Debbie was interested in Micah's work, and she plied him with questions while they ate a leisurely meal. It was easy for Laurel to remain silent and mull over this latest threat to her peace of mind. Although as Micah answered Debbie's queries, Laurel sensed his speculative gaze toward her.

"What's the most interesting place you've ever photographed?" Debbie asked.

"That's a hard one," Micah said. "I've been at this work a long time. I've had assignments all over the world."

"Do you speak several languages?" Laurel asked in an effort to keep Debbie from knowing how near the breaking point she was.

"French and Spanish reasonably well. I've picked up

a smattering of German, as well as a lot of Asian dialects—at least enough that I can find my way around in several countries."

At the dessert bar, Micah chose a large portion of apple cobbler, topped with a dollop of soft ice cream. Debbie took carrot cake, but Laurel picked up one cookie, wondering if she could eat it. The food she'd already eaten seemed like a lead weight in her stomach, and she felt nauseous. She desperately needed to be alone. The waitress brought Laurel and Micah fresh cups of coffee, and Debbie had a refill of iced tea.

"But you can't pick out a favorite place?" Debbie persisted, while they ate their desserts.

"Not on the spot like this. I'm always so busy looking forward to a new assignment that I rarely think about previous ones. I'll have to go through my scrapbooks and slide files and see if I can choose a favorite. Then perhaps I can revisit the area, and make a comparison of my impressions during my original research and what they are on my second visit."

"Seems like an excellent idea to me," Debbie said. She must have suddenly realized how quiet her mother had been, because Debbie covered Laurel's hand with hers. "Say, Mom, we're leaving you out of the conversation. I always talk too much. It's your turn to ask Micah some questions."

Laurel had noticed that Debbie and Micah had reached a first-name relationship right away. Determined that Debbie wouldn't notice her distress, Laurel forced a smile and said, "You're doing enough talking for both of us. But if Micah can't think of a favorite place he's photographed, I'll settle for one of the most exotic places he's explored."

"I have a large number of those to choose from," he said. "Machu Picchu comes to mind. You've heard of it?"

The name was familiar, but Laurel couldn't remember what or where it was.

"Some kind of an Inca site in Peru, right?" Debbie replied.

"Right. I went there about ten years ago. I rode a train from Cusco, Peru, to a little village at the foot of an Andean mountain where the historical site is located. I took a rickety bus along a narrow, curvy road to the top of the mountain. The driver handled that bus like he was driving a race car. After the ride *up* the mountain, I would have *walked* back down if it hadn't been for all the heavy equipment I had with me."

"Sorry to show my ignorance, but you two college graduates will have to refresh my memory on what Machu Picchu is," Laurel said, wishing as she often had before that she'd gone to college instead of getting married at eighteen.

"It's one of the most beautiful and perplexing sights I've ever seen," Micah said. "The Inca people carved hundreds of stone structures from the granite mountaintop in the fifteenth century. It was a self-contained city invisible from the valley below. When it was rediscovered in 1911 by Hiram Bingham, a Yale archaeologist, the jungle had taken over the site. Although the village is in ruins, enough of the dwellings are left to get an accurate idea of how the Incas lived and worshiped. I camped on the mountain one night and spent hours worshiping God, but after today's sermon, I'm not sure I worshiped Him in spirit and in truth."

Glancing at her watch, Debbie said, "I hate to break up our pleasant meal, but I have to be at work in an hour."

Micah stopped in his usual parking place, and before he went to his apartment, asked Laurel, "Do you still have the business card I gave you the day I arrived?"

Her face flushing, Laurel darted a quick glance at Debbie. "No. It was wet, and I threw it away."

Micah reached in his pocket, took out a card case and gave her another card. "My cell-phone number is on the card, so please feel free to call me if you need something. Did your cousin have reason to think you might be in some danger here?"

Laurel forced a laugh. "Of course not. We're perfectly safe."

But considering the telephone call and the letter in her purse, Laurel hoped her optimistic words had disguised her inner turmoil from Debbie and Micah.

"Cousin Kevin is a worrywart," Debbie said. "We have nothing to fear from our neighbors, and travelers wouldn't know there's a house out here."

"But you *are* isolated," Micah insisted, "so please

contact me if you need anything. I'll be here almost every night."

Micah's eyes revealed a warm tenderness and concern that made Laurel's heart beat faster. Knowing his strength and intelligence was at her beck and call gave her some assurance that she desperately needed.

Chapter Five

After thanking Micah for lunch, Debbie and Laurel walked upstairs side by side. Laurel kissed Debbie goodbye before she went into her bedroom.

"Lock the doors when you leave, dear. I may take a nap."

"Sure, Mom. You do look a little washed out. Please don't work so hard. We have several weeks before the wedding."

Laurel closed the bedroom door, stepped out of her shoes, released a pent-up breath and collapsed on the bed. Sleep and the work on her home were the furthest things from her mind. Many times during the past twenty years, while trying to provide for Debbie and deal with her in-laws, she'd experienced a lot of anxiety and fear, but she'd never faced anything like what was going on now.

She forced herself to lie immobile until Debbie went

downstairs. When she heard Debbie's car on the driveway, Laurel pushed a couple of pillows behind her back and reached for her purse.

She took out the envelope Kevin had brought her and smoothed out the single sheet of paper she'd crushed in her hands after reading the message.

"There is only a step between me and death. I Samuel 10:3."

Beneath the Bible quotation was a rough sketch of a skull and crossbones.

Who was harassing her? She supposed there were people who didn't particularly like her, but she couldn't think of anyone who disliked her enough to pull these practical jokes. If the messages were jokes. She started shaking as frightening images built in her mind. Was someone planning to kill her? Or worse, was Debbie in danger?

Laurel caught herself chewing her fingernails while she considered another puzzling incident that she hadn't connected with the phone call and letter before this. All the yard work and painting she'd done this spring had been hard on her nails, so she sat on her hands to keep them out of her mouth. When Micah had asked if it was dangerous for her to be alone at Oaklawn, she'd suddenly remembered an incident that hadn't concerned her at the time.

About two months earlier, she'd gone to a woman's retreat in Knoxville. On her return to Oaklawn at nine o'clock that evening, she'd had the intense feeling that some of the furniture in the hallway had been moved while she'd been gone. Debbie had been away for the weekend, and no one had keys to the house except Debbie and her, although they did keep a key hidden in the garage in case one of them lost her keys. *Had* someone been in the house that day? She hadn't been certain at the time, but now she was suspicious.

In an effort to block these bothersome thoughts from her mind, Laurel lay flat on the bed and focused on the morning church service and their meal with Micah. He'd seldom been out of her thoughts since he'd arrived at Oaklawn.

In her present state of mind, she didn't want to spend the evening alone. Would Micah think it strange if she invited him to eat with her when they'd just had lunch together? He'd told her to call if she needed him. She needed him now, but she couldn't tell him why. Panic-stricken at the thought of being alone until Debbie got home at midnight, she took Micah's business card out of her pocket. She dialed his number.

When he answered, she said, "Hello, this is Laurel. I'm in the mood for grilled hamburgers this evening and it's no fun picnicking alone. Do you want to join me in the picnic area near the rose garden?"

"I'd like that. I've been enjoying the view of your gardens from my kitchen window."

"Seven o'clock okay?"

"Yes. Don't go to a lot of trouble."

"No, I won't."

Laurel changed into a yellow gingham-checked blouse and a pink cotton split skirt. She loved shades of pink, but with her hair, she had to be sure she wore the colors below her waist. She prepared a vegetable salad and took hamburger patties out of the freezer to thaw. She gathered the condiments, bread and serving utensils and wondered what to do with her time until seven o'clock. She picked up her sewing basket and applied herself to her needlework.

Laurel was already at work at the grill when Micah arrived at the rose garden enclosed by a white paling fence. For a moment, he leaned on the half-open gate watching her. The evening sunlight, streaming through the foliage of a large oak tree, gleamed on her red curls.

Suddenly aware that she wasn't alone, Laurel swung around, her eyes wide and frightened. She smothered a gasp, and Micah thought she was going to faint. In one long stride, he was beside her, his arm circling her shoulders. Scanning her face worriedly, he helped her to a chair.

"I'm sorry I scared you."

Taking a steadying breath, she forced a smile to her lips. "You must think I'm terribly jumpy, but I was preoccupied, and I didn't hear you coming. You don't make any noise when you walk."

"It's a habit, I guess. When I'm photographing wildlife, I can't make a sound, or I'd miss some great pictures."

Micah had changed into a pair of khaki shorts and a white polo shirt. He wore white tennis shoes and ankle-length socks. As he hovered over her, she wondered why she'd ever thought that Micah wasn't a handsome man. His piercing blue eyes were the finest feature of his dark face. His firm nose and chin spoke of strength, yet she considered him the gentlest man she'd ever known. He had a high, intelligent forehead and the streaks of gray in his black hair set off his good looks. She'd known Micah only a few days. How could she have become so comfortable with him, as if she'd always known him?

Micah stirred a little under her intense scrutiny and, embarrassed, she glanced away. He turned his attention to the garden to give Laurel time to gain her composure. White-centered carmine-red buds marked the rambler roses cascading over the fence. A great hybrid ivory tea rosebush spread its branches across the wall of the brick house. Other varieties of roses that Micah didn't recognize were confined to a well-mulched bed in the middle of the garden. The blooming roses cast off a scent that reminded Micah of the sweet, exotic fragrance that seemed characteristic of Laurel. The grill, white picnic table and matching chairs were grouped near the kitchen door. Branching oak limbs shaded the garden from the hot rays of the sun.

A walk leading to a meadow-style garden was edged with brilliant yellow floribunda roses set inside lines of box-barberry. This garden was in open sun, which suited the Joe-Pye weeds—rather coarse, bold plants with purple-speckled stems, topped with mounds of mauve flower heads. Butterfly weeds with brilliant orange flowers attracted the monarch butterflies. Micah strolled along a walk of landscape stones, enjoying the buzzing bees and butterflies that surrounded him.

When he returned to the rose garden, Laurel had draped the picnic table with a dainty cloth and had placed three roses in an attractive triangular arrangement in a white pottery pitcher. Beef patties sizzled on the grill.

"Ah," Micah said as he sat in the chair Laurel indicated, sniffing the aroma of the juicy meat. "After that large lunch, I didn't think I'd want anything else to eat today, but I'm looking forward to a hamburger. It's nice of you to invite me."

Laurel flipped the patties once more to be sure they had cooked sufficiently before she turned off the gas. She sat opposite him at the table and passed the salad.

"Oh, but you're doing me a favor by eating with me," she said. "I didn't want to be alone tonight."

She hesitated, half tempted to tell Micah about the two frightening messages she'd had.

Micah saw the doubt and fear in her eyes and he thought she was going to confide in him, but instead, she said, "I have either lemonade or unsweetened iced tea to drink. Which would you rather have?"

"Lemonade, please."

She handed him a plate with a hamburger and bun

on it and placed a plate of dill pickles, sliced tomatoes, onions and lettuce within his reach.

"It's a fix-your-own-sandwich," she said, and the dimple beside her mouth deepened.

They didn't talk much while they ate, and when the meal was finished, Micah carried the utensils and serving dishes into the house while Laurel filled the dishwasher.

"Shall we sit in the garden?" she asked. "The weather is so special that I hate to spend any time indoors."

Micah hadn't known if he was expected to stay for a visit or if he'd just been invited for a meal, but he readily agreed to her suggestion. When they returned to the garden, Micah picked up the shears that Laurel had used to arrange the table decoration. He motioned toward a rose growing beside the garden gate.

"May I?" he asked. Her eyebrows lifted quizzically, but she nodded.

He went to the bush, inspected it for a few minutes before he cut off one of the large yellow rosebuds. He clipped the thorns from the stem. Smiling tenderly, he brought it to Laurel. His look of gentleness made her heart ache.

"Excuse the fact that my first flower to you is one of your own, but this is my thank-you for supper."

She colored, but she took the rose and sniffed its royal fragrance. Had he put an extra emphasis on the word "first"? Did he intend to give her other flowers? His next words answered her question.

"Although I doubt I'll find any flowers that equal yours in beauty, I'll *buy* the next flowers I give you."

"Thanks." She motioned to a chair opposite hers. "Sit down and 'smell the roses,'" she said in her quiet, musical voice.

Micah put a pillow behind his head and settled comfortably in the chair, his long legs crossed at the ankles and stretched out before him. When they'd come from the house, Laurel had brought a basket. She lifted some needlework from it.

"I'm making a counted cross-stitch sampler for Pastor Jensen and his wife. I want to have it finished for their silver anniversary in November, and I haven't made much progress. I do most of my needlework in the winter."

While Laurel worked, Micah enjoyed the serenity of the garden. He recognized various birdsongs coming from the trees around them. Butterflies flitted around their heads. Laurel was a picture of domesticity as she leaned over the work in her hands. He believed he could grow accustomed to this kind of living.

A ringing phone shattered the silence, and Laurel jumped, uttering a cry of distress. Icy fear twisted around her heart, and she started shaking. She couldn't have moved if she'd wanted to.

Micah stepped out of the lounge and started toward her.

"Answer it, please," she whispered.

Micah hurried into the kitchen and picked up the

phone, wondering what kind of message Laurel was expecting that had frightened her. He hesitated a moment before he answered.

"Hello."

After a momentary pause, the caller said, "This is Bruce Jensen. I was calling Laurel Cooper. Do I have the wrong number?"

"Oh, no, Pastor. Laurel is out in the rose garden. I'll call her."

"Is this Mr. Davidson?" Pastor Jensen said.

Momentarily, Micah thought the preacher might wonder what he was doing in Laurel's house. "Yes," he answered without an explanation.

"Just give Laurel a message. She volunteered to prepare a bouquet of flowers for one of our hospitalized members in Knoxville. Tell her I'll pick up the flowers around ten o'clock tomorrow morning. If she isn't going to be home, ask her to set them on the back porch."

Micah assured him that he'd give Laurel the message, and the pastor said, "I enjoyed having you at the church today. I hope to see you again at services."

Laurel sat motionless in her chair, her needlework lying in her lap.

"It was Pastor Jensen," Micah said immediately, and gave her the message. Her head bowed, and for a moment she remained in a frozen position.

"I don't want to be presumptuous since we've just met, but if you're having a problem, I'll be glad to help you."

Laurel stood, walked to the gate. She picked a rose from the rambler over the gate and shredded the fragrant bloom in her hand. The scent of the crushed blossom wafted toward Micah. She finally turned with a wan face, and the fear glimmering in her eyes disturbed Micah.

"I can't talk about it right now," she murmured.

Micah went to Laurel, took her hand and led her back to the chair. He knelt beside her, gently rubbing her hand.

"When you want to talk, I'm ready to listen. I think you need a break. Will you go with me tomorrow to research a house near Maryville? It's not a large house, but one worthy of being included in my article. We can easily make the trip in one day."

Her face lit at the prospect. "I'd love to go."

She didn't want to stay at Oaklawn, and she questioned if that was her harasser's motive. Was he trying to drive her away from her home? A day with Micah would be a godsend, but what if the man called and Debbie answered the phone?

"Maybe I'd better not," she said. "I have too much work to do. But I thank you for asking me."

Seeming embarrassed because she'd shown such panic in front of Micah, Laurel stood and Micah knew he'd been dismissed. Her face had that hopeless look he'd noticed the night before when she sat on the gallery. He believed the letter she'd gotten this morning had something to do with her problems. Was Kevin Cooper giving her some trouble?

Her hands unconsciously twisted together, and he thought she was close to tears. Micah thanked her for the food and reluctantly left. He compared Laurel's current manner to the vibrant woman she'd been when he first came to Oaklawn. How could she have changed so much in such a short time?

Not ready to go to his apartment, Micah walked down the oak-shaded drive toward the highway. Perhaps a fast walk would ease some of his frustrations. It was dark by the time he returned to the buildings. He wondered if Laurel was still in the garden, but he bypassed the house without stopping and went to his apartment.

As he turned on the light in his bedroom, he saw the Bible on the nightstand beside his bed. It had been there when he moved in, but he hadn't given it a second glance. After hearing the sermon this morning, he had a lot of unanswered questions, and he believed those answers were in the New Testament. He'd carried a small book of Psalms for years, and he'd read them often, but he had scant knowledge of the rest of the Bible. He took the Bible with him to the recliner in the living room and elevated his feet.

Looking for Scriptures to help him make the right connection between Jesus and the God of creation, Micah slowly turned the pages of the Bible. He noted certain passages that someone, presumably Laurel, had underlined.

One marked passage in the first chapter of the book of John seemed to jump off the page into his consciousness.

"Grace and truth came through Jesus Christ. No one has ever seen God, but God the only Son, who is at the Father's side, has made Him known."

What had Pastor Jensen said this morning? "God is spirit, and His worshipers must worship in spirit and in truth." So if grace and truth came through Jesus, then anyone who worshiped God must acknowledge the place of Jesus in God's plan.

Micah started reading the first chapter of John which dealt with the coming of the Word into the world. He read quickly through the whole chapter, realizing that the Word was a reference to Jesus. He paused and read aloud the first verse of the chapter. "'In the beginning was the Word, and the Word was with God, and the Word was God. He was with God in the beginning.'"

Slowly comprehending these words, he laughed softly. Jesus must have been present with God when the world was created. When he had worshiped the God of the Universe, the One who'd created the world, he hadn't realized that Jesus and the Father were one.

Without leaving his chair, Micah read the entire book of John. When he finished the last chapter, he felt as if he'd completed a marathon. If all of these words were true, and he believed they were, he had spent half of his life unaware of the necessity to receive Jesus as his Savior in order to have the right relationship with God.

Thoughtfully, Micah laid the Bible aside and prepared for bed. He hadn't understood many of the things he'd read. He would make an appointment to talk with Pastor Jensen to receive further enlightenment.

Micah had often read the twenty-second Psalm and had questioned who the psalmist had meant when he wrote, "Posterity will serve Him; future generations will be told about the Lord. They will proclaim His righteousness to a people yet unborn—for He has done it."

As he'd read the book of John tonight, Micah realized that the psalmist wrote about Jesus, Whom he'd ignored for so many years. If he claimed the truth that Jesus was the Son of God, how would that affect his relationship with Laurel? During their short acquaintance, he'd learned that Laurel's local church congregation was very important to her. Could he also make friends among these people?

The phone rang again as Laurel was in her room preparing for bed. Her hand hovered over the receiver. Was this another threatening call? Regardless of the extra cost, she must have Caller ID installed.

She picked up the phone, swallowed with difficulty and said, "Hello?"

"Hey, Mom," Debbie answered. "I'll have to work a double shift tomorrow. One of the other girls is sick, and I agreed to work extra. We could use the money."

"You don't have to do that," Laurel protested.

"I know, but I want to. I called so you wouldn't make any plans for us tomorrow."

"Micah asked me to go with him tomorrow while he researches a house for his article. I told him I wouldn't go."

"Why not? He's such a nice man, and a day off would be good for you. You've been working too hard anyway."

"We'll see."

Since Debbie would be away from home probably longer than she and Micah would be, there was little chance that her daughter would receive an intimidating phone call. The prospect of a day away from Oaklawn became more and more appealing to Laurel.

She dialed Micah's cell-phone number. When he answered quickly, she asked, "Am I calling too late?"

"No. I've been up reading."

"I'd like to change my mind and go with you tomorrow. Debbie phoned to say that she'll be working a double shift, so it seems like a good day for me to get away."

Briefly, he wondered what had happened to the pressing work she'd mentioned earlier. He was strangely elated that she'd accepted his invitation. He thought he had invited Laurel to go along to improve her mood, but now he wondered how much his personal happiness depended on Laurel's company.

"That will be great. We'll make a day of it. We can have dinner before we come home. Thanks for changing your plans to go with me."

"I've already picked the flowers and arranged the

bouquet for Pastor Jensen. I'll fix a few sandwiches and take some fruit along, so we can have a light lunch somewhere along the way."

"Thanks. Let's leave by eight o'clock."

Chapter Six

Laurel woke as excited about the day ahead of her as if she was going on a first date. Her leisurely bath added to her contentment, and she dressed in her newest outfit—a long, belted brown cotton skirt and a V-necked tan blouse. Considering the possibility of walking to where the house was located, she put on a sturdy pair of oxfords.

She and Debbie ate breakfast together, and Debbie asked, "Where are you going?"

"He said the house was near Maryville. I didn't intend to go, but I changed my mind when I knew you'd be out all day and evening."

Debbie drained the rest of her orange juice, kissed her mother's cheek, and said, "It will be midnight before I get home."

"I should think we'll be home long before that."

"Anyway, have a good time. And behave yourself,"

she said, teasingly. "Next thing I know, Micah will steal you away from me."

Laurel flushed, but she held Debbie's gaze. "Would you mind if I did marry again someday?"

"Of course not. Daddy has been gone for years. You should have remarried ages ago, but I sensed that Grandmother opposed it."

"I didn't ask that question because of Micah."

"Well, of course you didn't," Debbie said, and her eyes glinted with mischief.

"I didn't," Laurel said defensively. "But I've never lived alone, and I don't think I'll like it. After you marry and move, I might want some companionship."

"Now Mom, that's not the right reason to get married! Get a dog if all you want is company." Debbie put her arm around Laurel's shoulder and leaned her head against her mother's curly hair. "I want you to be happy. You've devoted yourself to making me happy. Now it's your turn. I have to get to work. 'Bye." Debbie turned away quickly, but Laurel saw that her eyes were misty when she left the kitchen. Was Debbie having second thoughts about moving so far away from Oaklawn?

Micah was punctual, as was Laurel, so they left Oaklawn at eight o'clock. As they drove away from the house, Laurel momentarily wondered what might be waiting for her when they returned. She drew a deep breath and forbade herself to be anxious about it. She intended to enjoy the day.

"Tell me what we're going to see," she said.

"A very unusual house located in the middle of the parking lot of a shopping center near Maryville."

"I think I heard about it on the news. The developer tried to move the house when they built the shopping center, right?"

"That's right. It's a two-story brick house from the early nineteenth century. I have an appointment to interview the African-American woman who lives there."

Although Laurel had seen the house on television, she was unprepared for the unique sight. When the owner refused to sell, the contractor built the shopping center around her half acre of land. A two-story brick house standing in the middle of a parking lot was an oddity!

Apparently undisturbed by the traffic and industry going on about her, Susanna Briggs sat on the back porch of the house waiting for them. Susanna was a small woman, about Laurel's height. She had serene black eyes that seemed to bear a constant twinkle. Her hair was gray, her face wrinkled. Laurel guessed she was in her eighties.

After she greeted them, Susanna said, "Go ahead and look the place over and take your pictures, then if you have any questions I'll answer them. I don't climb the stairs more'n I have to. I'll wait for you on the porch and look at my garden."

Susanna's small garden was behind the house, because at one time her home had stood directly upon the street, without a front yard. Built of unpainted red-colored bricks, the house had a front-to-back hall about seven feet wide with a large room on either side. A narrow flight of stairs led to the second floor also containing two large rooms. The kitchen and dining room were in a rear ell. The house had high, narrow proportions and an unbroken roof line without any portico. The roof was covered with slate shingles, and the exterior wood trim was painted yellow.

Laurel enjoyed watching Micah at work. He made notes on a palm-size computer. He was intent on his work, and she followed him silently. Accustomed to working alone, she thought that most of the time Micah forgot she was with him. Occasionally, he asked her to hold some of his equipment, but he obviously had a one-track mind when it came to his work.

It was almost noon when they finished the research and joined Susanna on the back porch. She motioned them to a rustic swing and passed a tray holding frosted glasses of lemonade.

"We brought our lunch with us," Laurel said to Susanna. "Will you share it with us?"

"That would be a treat," Susanna said. "You wouldn't think it, with all the bustle and stir that goes on around me twenty-four hours a day, but I do get lonesome sometimes. It's no fun to cook for one person, so mostly, I just eat snacks or soups."

Micah went to his car for the picnic basket Laurel had prepared, and Susanna brought a folding table from the house. Laurel had packed tuna salad sandwiches in an ice pack, cheese cubes, cookies, grapes and bananas.

Susanna rocked back and forth slowly, obviously enjoying their company and the food. While they ate, Micah and Laurel sat in the swing, their shoulders touching, listening to Susanna.

"My people came to Tennessee with Mr. Kilroy. He owned lots of land in these parts before the Civil War," Susanna said. "Maybe two-three thousand acres. He built this house when he first got married—some of his kids were born here. After he built a big house a few miles north along the river, he moved his family up there. My ancestor was Mr. Kilroy's personal servant— they'd more or less been brought up together, so Mr. Kilroy let my great-grandpa move in this house. It was a cut above what the other servants lived in."

"It was a wonderful house for that day and time," Micah said. "It's still in excellent repair."

Susanna beamed proudly. "And I aim to keep it that way. My ancestor went all through the war with Mr. Kilroy, and afore he died, the master willed this house to him and his assigns forever. Our family has lived in it ever since—just passed down from one generation to the other. I've been offered a lot of money for the site, but I don't aim to sell. I've got lots of grandkids, and one of them will want to live here when I'm gone." She chuckled, and her dark eyes gleamed.

Laurel could empathize with Susanna. She was trying to save Debbie's heritage for her, just as Susanna wanted to preserve the past for her descendants. Knowing that Susanna's efforts were more difficult than her own, Laurel was encouraged in her determination to keep Oaklawn.

Still, looking into the future, Laurel could see herself sitting alone year after year just as Susanna was. Not that she'd be in the center of a shopping center, but it would still be lonely.

"Do the owners of the shopping center harass you for not selling to them?" she asked, wondering again if her unwanted messages were intended to drive her out of her home. There had been some interest in expanding the campus of Walden College. If that should happen, a developer might have his eye on her property.

"Oh, at first, they were kinda snippy to me, but they knew I had my legal rights. They've accepted my living here. They'd thought I'd be bad for their business, but that ain't so. My house has become a tourist attraction. Hardly a day goes by, I don't have someone wanting to look at the place. I bet I get more Christmas presents than anyone else in the county. Somebody's always stopping by to give me something—even people I don't know."

She pointed to a restaurant several feet from her backyard. "I'm partial to their hamburgers, and the manager sends me over a hamburger and fries about every day."

"It would be a shame if this important part of history had been destroyed," Micah agreed.

"I don't think that'll ever happen," Susanna said, and her eyes were determined. "Just in case some of my relatives get greedy and decide to sell the place, I've made an airtight will. If none of my family will live here, the house will be deeded to the city of Maryville. I feel like I've got an obligation to preserve my heritage."

Laurel nodded understandingly. "I'm having the same problem—trying to keep a house for my daughter that she may never want to live in."

After Micah had gotten written permission from Susanna to use the interview and the photographs they'd taken, they got back into the car.

Micah glanced at his watch. "We're making such good time, why don't we drive over to Gatlinburg for our evening meal?"

"It's only two o'clock, and Debbie won't be home until midnight. We should have plenty of time."

"It's been years since I've been in the Blue Ridge Mountains, and I want to go before I finish this assignment. This seems like a good time."

"It is for me," Laurel agreed. "One last spree before the final preparations for the wedding."

As they left the town of Maryville behind them, Micah said, "You've mentioned finding a job after Debbie gets married. What kind of work do you have in mind?"

"I hardly know. I intend to start by taking a computer class at the college. I know it'll be difficult to get a job anyplace without computer skills. Debbie has a computer in her room, but I've never learned to use it. Since Dereck has a computer, too, Debbie will leave hers for me. She wants to be able to contact me by e-mail."

They approached Gatlinburg from the west, and Micah drove leisurely as they approached the mountains. The traffic increased as they entered the town, and Micah took the first parking space he could find.

"We'll see more if we walk around," he said. They walked along the crowded streets for an hour, window-shopping, and occasionally going inside a building to watch craftsmen at work. Micah remarked on the many wedding chapels they saw. They stopped at Christus Gardens where they enjoyed the interior gardens and saw the dramatically lit, life-size figures depicting the life of Christ. They got into the car and left Gatlinburg, stopping at a restaurant in Pigeon Forge for dinner.

As they started their return to Oaklawn, Laurel leaned her head back against the seat. She'd developed an interest in Micah, unlike any she'd known before. The few dates she'd had several years ago were mostly with men she'd known for years, and she'd accepted their invitations mostly to get out of the house.

Being with Micah was different. She was at ease with him. Although she'd loved Jason, he wasn't an easy man to live with. She'd never felt free to divulge her innermost thoughts to her husband. She was tempted to tell Micah about the threatening phone call and letter, but she didn't want to spoil the day by discussing her fears.

After Micah left Laurel at her door, he was too restless to settle for the night. Several times during his sojourn in South America, he'd contemplated following a less active lifestyle. Especially after he'd received an invitation to work at Walden College, he'd wondered if it was time for him to settle down. Even then, he hadn't gone as far as to think of marriage. He'd mostly thought of living on his acreage in Kansas, although the idea wasn't appealing. Several times lately he'd contemplated what marriage to Laurel would be like. Had he lived alone too long to include another person in his life? And it was apparent that Laurel wouldn't leave Oaklawn. He'd always thought living in one area would be boring. Smiling, he knew if he became bored, all he'd have to do would be to spark Laurel's temper, and things would get lively in a hurry.

He was emotionally drawn to Laurel, but was he cut out to be a husband? A mental flash reminded him of a wild mustang trapped behind a fence. He liked the freedom to do what he wanted to when he wanted to, without considering anyone else. But if he was around Laurel much longer he was bound to do something foolish. Should he cut his ties with Oaklawn and find another apartment?

"Out of sight, out of mind," he'd always heard. If he didn't see Laurel anymore, his obvious attraction to her would soon fade. But was leaving her the coward's way out? Wasn't he man enough to withstand his feelings for Laurel? Why leave a convenient apartment because he couldn't control his emotions?

"Loaf one day and work hard the next one," Laurel thought as she knelt on the linoleum floor putting a new coat of paint on the kitchen cabinets. Yesterday with Micah had been the most wonderful time she'd had for years. His quiet, understanding manner had calmed her worries, but once she was away from him, she couldn't get the frightening call and letter out of her mind.

Her thoughts were interrupted by a knock on the screen door, and her hands shook as she laid the brush carefully on top of the can. Her hand clutched her pulsing throat, wondering if her harasser was at the door. She'd taken the precaution of locking the screen door so no one would catch her unawares.

Last night she'd had a dream—more like a nightmare—when she thought someone was watching her. She'd whirled around, and a masked face was peering in the window at her. She'd awakened with the terrible feeling that she was trapped.

The knock came again, and she grabbed hold of the sink top to pull herself up. She remembered a quotation she'd read a few days ago— "We must travel in the direction of our fear." She wiped her hands on a damp cloth, muttering a Bible verse that she'd memorized this morning. "God has not given us the spirit of fear— but of power, and of love, and of a sound mind."

If God hadn't given her the spirit of fear, then she wished her legs knew about it. On trembling knees, she moved toward the door. Her breath caught in her throat, and oozed out in a sigh of relief when she saw Cousin Kevin.

"I was beginning to think you weren't at home," he

said. "Debbie told me you'd gone off for the day yesterday with Mr. Davidson, but I thought perhaps I'd mistaken the day."

Unlatching the door, she said, "We were away yesterday, so I'm working extra hard today."

"Then maybe I shouldn't bother you."

She thought he'd already bothered her and wished he'd called, letting her know he'd wanted to stop by. But she said graciously, "No. Come in. I need to take a break. We'll sit in the kitchen, if you don't mind. I may have paint on my shoes, and I don't want to track up the rest of the house."

"The kitchen is fine," Kevin said, with a smile. "Maybe I can beg a cup of coffee?"

"Of course. Sit down." Laurel washed her hands at the sink. Sniffing, she said, "The paint smell is pretty strong. Maybe you'd prefer sitting on the porch?"

"No, I'm all right. The paint smell isn't offensive— just a nice clean scent."

She set two cups on the table and reached in the refrigerator for milk. She drank her coffee black, but Kevin preferred a drop or two of milk in his cup.

"I made coffee cake for breakfast. Would you like a slice?"

"That would be great. Actually, I skipped breakfast this morning."

Laurel served Kevin a large portion of the cake and sat across the table from him. She never had to do much to entertain Kevin, since he liked to talk about his work.

She sipped slowly on her coffee. After the death of his wife, he and his two girls always came to Oaklawn for Christmas and other holidays while his children were growing up. Now that his children had married, he spent the holidays with them.

After he finished the cake, Kevin got up and poured another cup of coffee from the carafe near the sink.

"You're a good cook, Laurel. That cake was delicious."

"Well, thank you," she said, with a smile. "But you'll have to give Betty Crocker most of the credit. All I did was mix an egg and some milk with the dry ingredients and put the batter in the oven."

"Then thanks to both you and Betty," he said affably.

When he settled back in his chair, apparently with no notion of leaving, Laurel got up, put the paintbrush in a jar of water and tapped the lid in place on the paint can.

"A client has approached me to find out if you'd be interested in selling Oaklawn."

"What! Who?"

"I can't answer your question, as the client wants to remain anonymous. That's the reason he came to me instead of contacting you personally, but I assure you the offer is on the up-and-up."

"You know I can't sell Oaklawn. Debbie's grandparents deeded the property to me when they died, because she wasn't of age, and they thought that was the best way to handle it. I'm surprised you didn't tell your client that the estate isn't for sale."

He shrugged his shoulders. "I didn't feel I had that right without asking you. I know you're having quite a struggle to keep going here."

"Would you want to see anyone other than Coopers owning the estate? After all, it's part of your heritage, too."

"Oh, I'm flexible about these things. Since I don't have a son, and you have only Debbie, Oaklawn will eventually go out of the Cooper name anyway. Debbie should have been a boy."

Was this the cause of the harassment? Did someone want to buy Oaklawn, and they were trying to scare her away so they could get the property at a low price?

Kevin cleared his throat nervously, and he stammered a few times, which surprised Laurel, because he was never at a loss for words.

"There is something I've been meaning to talk to you about, Laurel. The time has never seemed right, but now that Debbie is leaving and you're going to be alone, I've wondered if the two of us might get together."

Laurel stared at him. She'd never suspected that he had any romantic interest in her. How long had Kevin been entertaining such thoughts? Then as he continued, she decided it wasn't romance he was interested in, but a way to continue the Cooper line.

"Well, what I mean…we aren't too old yet to… well, to have some children together. If we'd get married, both our problems would be solved. I have the finances to help you with the upkeep of Oaklawn, and if we had a son, the property could stay in the Cooper family."

Laurel's eyes narrowed a little, and she felt her dander rising, because she was angry as well as amused. She didn't want to offend Kevin, but she thought he was completely out of line.

"In your plans, Kevin, you're overlooking one very important point," she said sharply. "My in-laws left Oaklawn to me for the sole purpose of passing it on to Debbie. Yes, *Debbie*, not some other child I might conceive, even if the child was a Cooper. And even though Debbie is going to change her name when she's married, she was born a Cooper, and she'll remain a Cooper until the day she dies."

"How do you know she'll ever want to live here?"

"I don't know that. If she doesn't, *she* can sell Oaklawn. I certainly won't place any restrictions on her."

"Finding a buyer for a place like this isn't easy."

"Oh, I don't know. You just said you have a potential buyer." Laurel supposed she should be happy to have a chance to get out from under the burden of Oaklawn. However, faced with the thought of leaving the place that had been her home for more than half of her life, she knew she was tied to this home with cords that couldn't easily be broken.

"You've spent a lot of money on this place and there will be constant upkeep as the years go by."

"That will be Debbie's problem, not mine. All I need to do is keep Oaklawn in good shape until she decides what to do with it. As for having a child, if you think, at my age, that I'd enjoy being pregnant, having morning sickness, and start nighttime feedings, diaper changing, potty training and all the other 'joys' of parenthood, you must be out of your mind. If I had a son today, I'd be drawing Social Security by the time he finished college."

"I didn't mean to upset you."

"I know that, but you should be able to see what a ridiculous idea it is."

"Then that means you won't marry me."

"Of course not," she said indignantly. "I realize you think it's a probable solution to my financial problems, and perhaps it is, but you're too much like family for me to marry you. Just go on being my friend and cousin—that's what I need from you."

"It was just a thought," he said, with only a minimum of regret sounding in his voice.

He held out his hand and she placed her hand in his.

"No hard feelings?" he asked.

"No. I'm flattered. I thought I was past the age when I'd receive a marriage proposal."

He laughed slightly. "You might be receiving lots of proposals now that Debbie is getting married."

As he took his leave, she wondered if that had been the reason he'd proposed. Was he afraid she would marry someone else and bring him to Oaklawn to live? She waved goodbye, bemused over Kevin's suggestion.

Laurel returned to her painting. Absentmindedly, she smoothed the pale yellow enamel over the wooden doors. When she glanced at the clock and saw that it was almost noon, she knew she'd have to wake Debbie soon. After working sixteen hours yesterday, she was no doubt plenty tired.

But about the time she finished painting, she heard water running and knew that Debbie had gotten up. She cleaned away the paint things and prepared a tomato and cottage-cheese salad for their lunch. She stirred lemonade mix into chilled water and set it in the refrigerator. While some leftover vegetable soup simmered, she set the table in the dining room, rather than eating their lunch with the smell of paint all around them.

Debbie, looking neat and lovely in the short red skirt and white blouse uniform she wore at work, yawned and stretched when she came into the kitchen.

"Still sleepy, honey?" Laurel asked.

"Yes, I am, but I'll be more awake once I start eating." When they sat at the table, Debbie asked, "How was your day yesterday?"

"Wonderful! We saw the most interesting old brick house, and the owner is a dear person. After Micah finished his photographs and interview, we drove on to Gatlinburg and looked around a little before we had dinner. I hadn't been home more than an hour when you came in."

"So we were both night owls, huh?"

"Late hours won't hurt me once in a while."

As they ate their meal, Laurel told Debbie about the Kilroy home and more details of their day.

"What else is new?" Debbie asked, as she lifted a spoonful of steaming soup to her mouth.

Mischievously, Laurel said, "I received a marriage proposal this morning."

Debbie's soup went down the wrong way. She choked and reached for her glass of lemonade.

"Who from? Micah?"

Amazed that Debbie had immediately jumped to that conclusion, Laurel protested, "No! I hardly know the man. It was from Cousin Kevin."

"That surprises me even more," Debbie said, clearing her throat. "Marrying him would be about like marrying your brother, wouldn't it?"

"That's what I told him. And don't think he's harboring any passionate feelings for me. He suggested a marriage of convenience—he'd have the money to keep up Oaklawn, and I'd provide him a son who could inherit the property."

"You're kidding!"

Laurel held up her right hand. "Scout's honor! I rejected his offer and reminded him that you're the one who will inherit Oaklawn."

"He knows that as well as you do. Why would he suggest such a thing?"

"He has a client who wants to buy Oaklawn. That may have prompted his concern. Perhaps he was worried I might sell the estate out of the family."

"Did he name the potential buyer?"

"No, a matter of client/attorney secrecy." Laurel drummed her fingers idly on the table. The phone rang, and she jumped.

Debbie said, "I'll get it," but Laurel shook her head and rushed into the kitchen. As much as possible, she intended to screen all calls. Soon, with an inward feeling of relief, she gave the phone to Debbie.

After a brief conversation, Debbie clicked the Off button on the phone and laid it on the table.

"That was my friend, Ashley. Her car is in the garage and she wants me to pick her up and take her to work."

Glancing at the clock and noting that Debbie didn't have to leave for over an hour, Laurel said, "I've never asked you this, so I will now. Do you think you'll ever want to live at Oaklawn? Or would you prefer to sell the place and invest the money in a home of your own?"

Debbie chewed slowly on a cracker before she answered.

"I don't know, Mom. As far as I'm concerned, Oaklawn is yours as long as you live. You make the decisions of whether to keep it or sell it. Right now, Oaklawn is home to me and will be, no matter where I move to. But it's home because *you're* here. If you were no longer living, I don't know whether I'd ever want to live in the house."

Touched by her daughter's devotion, Laurel's throat was a bit tight when she answered. "Well, it isn't a decision we have to make now. I have no intention of selling Oaklawn or of marrying Kevin. I thought it was a ridiculous suggestion, and I told him so."

"But Mom, the idea of you marrying again isn't a *bad* one. I feel terrible to go off and leave you here alone, and I'd like to see you married. So if you do fall in love with someone, I'm all in favor of it."

"Thanks for telling me. I won't marry someone just because I'm lonely and want a companion. But if I find someone to love, I'll certainly consider it."

She'd married in haste the first time because her grandmother was dying, and she'd wanted to see Laurel settled before she died. She had learned to love Jason, but she hadn't when she agreed to marry him. She was interested in Micah, but she didn't know if she loved him. But it was good to have Debbie's blessing if she should decide to remarry.

Chapter Seven

Micah had mixed emotions about his interview at the college. There were advantages to having a nine-to-five job, but it distressed him to even consider giving up his active, rigorous, stimulating lifestyle without ties or obligations. But the past year, he'd sensed something was missing in his life—that there was more to life than fame and adventure. Since he'd started reading the Bible, he'd realized that part of his problem was spiritual. But he'd been dissatisfied for several months before he came to Tennessee.

He had two hours before his appointment at the college, and he set out for a walk to the river. When had his dissatisfaction started? As he strolled, feeling a slight breeze on his face, and the sun warming his back, he dated his discontent to almost two years ago, before he'd gone to South America. One of his nieces was being married, and since he was between assignments, he'd gone to the wedding. It was the first time he'd been with all of his immediate family for years, and he'd felt like a fifth wheel. His two sisters and his brother were all married and had families that totaled thirty-six. Over two hundred people attended the wedding, because his sister and brother-in-law, as well as his niece and her new in-laws, had many friends.

Not only had he remained single, but he hadn't even gathered many friends. He hadn't stayed in any one place long enough to get close to anyone.

He'd soon be fifty, and he had no illusions that he wanted to start a family of his own. It wouldn't be fair to children to have a father old enough to be their grandfather. His only option was to acquire a ready-made family like Laurel and Debbie. Since he'd been at Oaklawn, he'd noticed the close relationship and affection between them and had wondered what it would be like to be the recipient of such devotion.

Why had he been drawn to Laurel more than other women he'd met? She had a quick mind, and she faced her problems with courage and resolution. She was tenderhearted but hot-tempered. Her fiery temperament appealed to him. And when her well-shaped mouth curved into a quick smile of repentance after her anger passed, he was hard put to keep from snatching her in his arms and kissing her. Such an action wasn't to be considered until he was confident he could "stay in the harness once he got hitched," as one of his Western cronies often said.

Returning to his apartment, he saw Laurel working in the flower garden. With her back to him, she was on her knees pulling weeds and spraying the roses. He leaned on the fence, watching her for a few minutes. Once, her hands stilled at her tasks, and she looked across Oaklawn's borders to the mountains beyond. From the rigid set of her shoulders, he knew she wasn't observing the beauty of nature.

He didn't want to startle her, so he quietly retraced his steps. When he was out of sight, he started whistling. Arriving at the fence the second time, Laurel looked his way.

"Good morning," he said. "You're up early."

"It's going to be hot today, and I wanted to do some yard work before the sun's rays reach this corner of the garden. Have you been walking?"

"Yes, to the river. I have some things to do in this area today, so I didn't have to start out early."

He didn't know why he didn't tell her that he might start working at the college. He supposed it was because he wasn't used to telling his plans to anyone. This was another thing for him to consider. After being a bachelor for years, would he be able to take anyone wholeheartedly into his life?

"I've finished what I planned to do. Do you have time to come in for a cup of coffee?"

"No, I can't now, but I'll take a rain check on the invitation."

She smiled brightly at him, as if she didn't have a

care in the world, but her expression often changed from bright to cloudy in a moment. He wished he knew the reason for her rapid mood swings.

His walk across the college campus reminded Micah of his days as a student. He'd lectured at many colleges since then, but Walden College was more like the one he'd attended as a young man.

The century-old stone buildings were set in a campus of large maple and oak trees. Squirrels scampered across his path and mockingbirds chattered sassily from the shrubbery. Apparently there was no air-conditioning in the buildings, because the windows were open. Summer classes were in session, and he heard the murmur of voices as he passed several buildings on his way to the administrative offices.

Micah's appointment was with the president, Silas Decker. Decker was younger than Micah, but had been associated with the college for ten years.

"Mr. Davidson," he said, "we're flattered that you're considering joining our staff."

"As I told you when we discussed this by phone, I'm not sure I'm ready to become a full-fledged professor. But since I was coming to Tennessee on this assignment, it seemed like a good opportunity to talk with you about it. Even if I do accept an appointment here, I'm sure I'd prefer a part-time job at first. I enjoy doing lecture series, but I may not be ready for a full-time professorship."

"We have no objections if you want to ease into the work gradually."

"I'd like to look around the campus and sit in on some classes to get a feel for the student body and the teaching staff. I'm staying in the area through the summer. If you'll prepare a prospectus for both a part-time job and a full-time one, then it will give me something to consider."

"If you'll leave your address, I'll take care of that this week and mail it to you."

"I live nearby, and I'll pick up the prospectus. Can I let you know my decision by the first of September?"

"Yes. If you accept, we'll schedule you for classes in the winter quarter, starting in January."

Two weeks passed without any phone calls or messages by mail, and Laurel stopped jumping every time the phone rang. Micah continued to go with them to church on Sunday morning, and afterward the three of them went to lunch together. Laurel was pleased when Micah arranged for some counseling sessions with Reverend Jensen. She wasn't sure in what direction their relationship was heading, but she knew that Micah's enlightenment of the Scriptures would be a deciding force in her acceptance of him as a future mate.

Then another letter came, and again it contained a hand-printed Scripture verse.

"A time to be born, and a time to die."

The caption on this message showed a woman holding a child, and it upset her more than the others. Was this man a threat to Debbie? Laurel couldn't put the thought out of her mind, and she started staying up until Debbie came home. Two nights after she received the letter, the phone rang about midnight.

Concerned about Debbie, Laurel snatched the phone from the table without thinking about her harasser. She screamed when a man started singing, "She'll be comin' around the mountain when she comes."

"Leave me alone!" she shouted. "I'm calling the police." Her hands shook wildly as she slammed down the receiver.

The phone rang again almost immediately, and she snatched it up. "Stop calling me!"

"Mom?" Debbie said. "It's me. Who did you think was calling?"

Sick with relief to hear Debbie's voice, Laurel said, "I'd just had a prank call, and I thought he was phoning again. Where are you?"

"I had a wreck."

"What!"

"Somebody forced me off the highway, and I'm stranded in a ditch. I'm all right, but I'm waiting for a tow truck."

"Where?"

"About five miles west of our driveway."

"I'll come right away."

"That isn't necessary—" Debbie started, and Laurel interrupted.

"I'll be there."

Laurel was shaking so much, she didn't think she could drive safely, but she had to see for herself that Debbie was all right. She looked out the window, and Micah's light was still on. She called him.

"Oh, Micah. Debbie's had a wreck, and I don't think I'm fit to be driving. Will you take me?"

"As soon as I put my shoes on. Is she hurt?"

"She called and said she isn't. She's only five miles down the highway."

"Meet me at my car."

Laurel grabbed her purse, locked the door after her, and reached the car only seconds before Micah came running toward her. After he opened the car door for Laurel and fastened her seat belt because her hands were shaking too much to accomplish the task, Micah hurried into the driver's seat and sped out of the driveway. Ten minutes after Debbie had called, they arrived at the scene of the accident.

An ambulance, fire truck and a squad car were all there before them, and the tow truck pulled in behind Micah's car. Laurel ran to Debbie, who was being checked by an EMT.

"Now, Mom, I'm all right," Debbie assured her, but Laurel snatched her into a close embrace for a minute. Then she stood back and waited until the EMT had finished.

Micah went immediately to check Debbie's car, and he soon reported, "There doesn't seem to be much damage except to your right bumper and headlight. You have insurance, don't you?"

"Yes," Debbie said. "The papers are in the glove compartment."

"Do you feel like talking to the police now, Debbie?" Micah asked. "They have a lot of questions."

When Debbie assured him she was all right, he said to Laurel, "Why don't you come with me. We can get the registration and insurance information out of the car and you can tell the tow-truck driver where you want the car taken for repair. Although you'll probably need more than one estimate."

Micah didn't like the haunted look in Laurel's eyes, and he wanted to give her something to do. Within an hour, the car had been pulled from the ditch and was on its way to a garage in Knoxville. The police had finished their investigation, although Debbie couldn't give them much information about who had forced her off the road, except that it was a car rather than a truck or van. Her vital signs were satisfactory, so it wasn't necessary for her to go to the hospital. They didn't return to Oaklawn until two o'clock in the morning.

"I'm beginning to feel some sore places now," Debbie admitted as she stepped carefully from the car. Micah held her arm and walked her upstairs to her bedroom.

"A hot bath will make you feel better," Laurel said. "I'll run the water for you."

After he'd delivered Debbie to her room, Micah said, "I'll brew some decaf tea and bring you a cup, Debbie."

"Thanks," Debbie said and kissed him on the cheek. "I don't know what we'd have done if you hadn't taken charge. I'm still shaking."

"A night's rest will help you," Laurel said. "Micah, save some tea for me. I'll be down as soon as Debbie's in bed."

A half hour later, Laurel entered the kitchen where Micah waited for her. He poured tea into a mug, and she said, "Let's sit on the back porch. I don't want Debbie to hear what I say."

She sat in her favorite lounge chair and Micah pulled a chair close to her, so she could talk quietly. She sipped slowly on the tea, and he listened without interrupting as she told him of the phone calls and notes she'd received over the past month. "The first call was the day you came to Oaklawn, and the last one was a few minutes before Debbie had her wreck." Her voice shook as she added, "I think someone tried to kill her."

"Since the first call was on the day I came, did you suspect me?" he asked, amusement in his voice.

"At first, I wondered if it could be you, but after I heard you singing, I *knew* it wasn't you," she said with a small smile.

In the dim light from the hallway, she saw him lift quizzical eyebrows. "You haven't heard me sing."

"You were humming that day when we walked back from the river, and you have a deep bass voice. This guy is a tenor. Although the voice seems disguised, I don't suspect you."

"Why haven't you contacted the police?"

"I don't want Debbie to know about it, or she might feel obligated to stay at home instead of going ahead with her marriage plans. Besides, until now I've hoped the messages might be from some kid who was having fun at my expense. I thought they might eventually stop without having to make a public issue of it."

Micah stood up, took Laurel's hand and pulled her upward into a snug embrace. "You don't have to bear this burden by yourself. I'm here to help you, and we'll find out what's going on."

She snuggled close to him, enjoying the feel of his arms around her. She'd been on her own for twenty years, and it was comforting to hear Micah say that he would help her. She would have liked to prolong the embrace forever, and she wondered if she was falling in love with Micah.

With a weary sigh, she pulled away and caressed his face. "I'll welcome any help you can give me. Mostly, though, it just helps to have someone to confide in. I've been terribly worried. I hope I can keep Debbie from knowing. I don't want to ruin her last summer at home."

Micah took the hand she held against his face and kissed it. "Go to bed, Laurel. I'll be a little more vigilant about what's going on at your house. If you won't call the police, at least promise to tell me anything else that happens."

"I promise. I'm relieved to have someone else know what's going on."

* * *

The next few days passed without any troubling messages, and Laurel and Debbie continued with plans for the wedding. Laurel also shopped for draperies for the parlor and entrance hall, but with the high ceilings in her house, draperies had to be custom-made and the prices were high.

One morning when they were shopping in a gift shop for wedding favors, Debbie drew Laurel's attention to a display of "Over the Hill" birthday decorations. "Over the Hill" in this case meant people who were celebrating their fiftieth birthdays.

Laurel picked up a card featuring an exhausted man placing a flag on the mountain he'd just climbed. The inside illustration showed an avalanche striking the man and hurtling him down the hill. The caption said, "You made it to the top. It's faster and easier going downhill."

While they laughed at the display of cards, Laurel said, "I just remembered something. When Micah first came, he mentioned that he'd be fifty at the end of June. Let's surprise him with an 'Over the Hill' party."

"Sounds like fun, Mom. He's been good to us, and I figure we owe him a party. But can you take on anything else this summer?"

"I might be able to, if my daughter helps. Besides, everything is finished for the wedding, except for last-minute things."

"I can make sandwiches and get some snack foods. But who would we invite?"

"Since the idea is only two minutes old, I hadn't thought about that. He doesn't know anyone in the community except our church family, so I suppose we could invite the whole congregation. Micah seems to feel at ease with them."

"Then let's do it."

"Yes. He's been helpful, doing things around the house for me. Last week when he had a free afternoon, he insisted on mowing the lawn. I'll feel guilty taking his rent payment for next month."

"Let's not buy any decorations until we make a few more plans," Debbie said.

Laurel agreed, and Debbie said, "I can pick them up anytime when I'm going to work."

As they were driving home, Debbie asked, "What day of the week is Micah's birthday?"

Laurel checked the pocket-size yearly calendar in her purse. "Sunday."

"Oh, that's perfect. We can have a cookout right after church."

"That would be a lot of food for us to prepare. I'm not sure we can afford it," Laurel said.

"We'll provide the beverages, burgers, hot dogs, rolls and condiments, and ask our guests to bring a vegetable, salad or a dessert. I'm sure Mrs. Jensen would make a small birthday cake as her contribution. We'll tell everyone not to bring gifts, so they won't mind helping with the food."

"I'll mention the surprise party at our women's circle meeting next Thursday afternoon. Most of our families will have a representative there, and I'll ask the ones who attend to spread the word."

Micah didn't seem to suspect a thing when he joined Laurel on Oaklawn's portico the night before his party. The day had been extremely hot, but a western breeze made the evening pleasant and cool. A full moon rose in a cloudless sky, and the fragrance of roses perfumed the twilight air.

"Debbie and I want to grill hamburgers for lunch tomorrow," Laurel said. "Why don't you join us? You've been treating us to Sunday lunch, now it's our turn."

"I'd like that. I'm leaving on Monday for a few days in New York City. I'm working with a publisher who's putting out a book on my two-month hiking trip in Tibet and Nepal. We have to come to an agreement about which pictures to use."

"How much more do you have to do on your magazine assignment?"

"I've pretty much finished in this section of Tennessee. But I have several houses to visit in the western part of the state. I should be through by the last week in August."

After Micah's comforting presence all summer, Laurel dreaded his departure. "Then if I have a request for the apartment, you won't be needing it after August."

Reluctant to break his ties with Oaklawn, Micah squirmed in his chair and said, "I wouldn't want you to lose a tenant, but I would like to reserve at least through September."

He wasn't even comfortable about leaving Laurel to go to New York, so how could he leave her permanently? If he accepted the job at the college, he could stay at Oaklawn, but he knew he couldn't make such a momentous decision just because he wanted to stay with Laurel.

Relieved that she wouldn't be losing Debbie and Micah at the same time, Laurel said lightly, "Oh, that's no problem. If someone wants the apartment, I can always put the person in one of our spare bedrooms until the apartment is available. I've done that before."

She'd been busier than usual preparing for Micah's party, but sitting on the portico for an hour rested Laurel. She was still tired but happy when she told Micah good-night and climbed the steps to her bedroom.

When the phone rang at midnight, she was startled from a sound sleep. Cold fear gripped her when she sat up and saw what time it was. She considered not answering, but she hadn't heard Debbie come in, so she couldn't take any chances.

Besides, she couldn't fight fear by running from it, so she leaned on her left elbow and lifted the receiver. She didn't say anything, nor did her caller. After a few seconds, a fiendish laugh sounded in her ears. The caller severed the connection before Laurel could.

She turned on the light and walked down the hall to

see if Debbie was home. She was, and Laurel returned to her room and disconnected the phone. Sleep was over for the night, and she sat in a chair and rocked slowly, trying to make some sense out of the situation. If she didn't believe that God was faithful in His promises to sustain His followers, she didn't know what she would do.

She reached for her Bible and turned to the Ninety-First Psalm. The rest of the night, she meditated on the words of the psalmist and his confidence that those who served God were never beyond His encompassing care.

Several times she read aloud the last verses of the Psalm. "'I will protect him, for he acknowledges My name. He will call upon Me, and I will answer him; I will be with him in trouble. I will deliver him and honor him. With long life will I satisfy him and show him My salvation.'"

After Laurel assured Micah that they didn't need any help preparing for the cookout the next day, he went to his apartment to change into shorts and a polo shirt. Two counseling sessions with Pastor Jensen had gone a long way toward convincing Micah that he had been wrong in believing that accepting God as the Creator of the universe was all God expected of His followers. The pastor's message this morning had confirmed his need to accept Jesus as his Savior and Lord of his life.

As he reviewed the pastor's text from the eighth

chapter of Romans, Micah realized that it was only a step from where he was now spiritually to becoming the kind of person God wanted him to be.

He opened the Bible and turned to a passage Pastor Jensen had read during the service. "If you confess with your mouth, 'Jesus is Lord,' and believe in your heart that God raised Him from the dead, you will be saved. For it is with your heart that you believe and are justi-fied, and it is with your mouth that you confess and are saved."

Micah knelt by his bed. "Jesus, I confess You as my Savior and Lord. Send the Holy Spirit to dwell in my heart and make me the kind of follower You can use."

Suddenly he realized that it was his fiftieth birthday, and he smiled. How fitting that in the future when he celebrated the day of his natural birth, he could also re-member his spiritual birthday.

Since he'd lived a solitary life for many years, Micah supposed it was appropriate that when he made the most important decision of his life he would be alone. He would soon share his decision with the pastor and Lau-rel, but when his mind turned to her, he was troubled.

She had been preoccupied during the worship ser-vice. Her hands had shaken when she held the hymn book, and her body was tense. When the congregation had prayed the Lord's Prayer, he detected a tremor in her voice. He'd had a few minutes alone with her be-fore Debbie came to the car, and she'd told him in a hushed whisper that she'd had another call.

That news had set off alarm bells in Micah's mind. He knew she didn't want anything to upset Debbie's wedding, but how much longer could he stand aside while someone threatened Laurel's life?

The guests were coming at one o'clock, and Laurel hurried to change into light blue pants and shirt before she carried the black plates, napkins and cups to the picnic table and covered them with a tablecloth to hide them. She had started the gas grill and was carrying out a container of ice when Micah sauntered into the garden.

Seeing that Laurel was alone, he asked what had happened last night. She told him quickly, and he said, "We can't let this go on much longer. We need to contact the police or at least get the telephone company to trace the calls."

She didn't have time to respond as Debbie came out of the house carrying a plastic tablecloth from the house. "Hey, Micah," she said, "help me spread this on the serving table."

Micah had his back to the garden gate when Pastor Jensen peered over the fence and beckoned his parishioners to come closer. In a loud chorus, they shouted, "Happy 'Over the Hill' birthday, Micah."

The surprise on Micah's face was ludicrous as he whirled to face them. Astonished, he turned to Laurel.

"How did you know?"

Laughingly, she said, "The day you came to Oaklawn, you mentioned that you'd have your half-century birthday on the last day of June. It seemed like a good excuse to have a party."

"I haven't celebrated my birthday for years, but thanks."

Eyes alight with an expression that made her blood tingle, Micah squeezed her hand before he walked to the gate and greeted everyone as they entered the garden. Not only did they bring food, but they had their lawn chairs, folding tables and two more grills. In a short time, more than fifty people had gathered in the garden area. While several of the women helped Laurel and Debbie organize the food, Pastor Jensen, Kevin Cooper and another man took charge of cooking the meat.

Seeing that many people were carrying greeting cards, Laurel brought a basket and set it on the corner of the serving table to hold the cards. She had a feeling that Micah hadn't had a lot of personal attention in his life, and it was heartwarming to see her church family gathering Micah into the fellowship. So much food had been brought that Laurel had Cousin Kevin bring out a folding table from the basement to display the food.

The pastor's wife had made a chocolate cake with dark chocolate icing, and she'd placed fifty black candles on it.

It took four attempts before Micah blew out all the candles.

No one seemed to be in a hurry to leave, but at four

o'clock, Debbie said, "Everyone, I have to leave for work. Thanks for coming and continue to have fun."

Kevin looked at his watch and jumped to his feet. "Four o'clock!" he said. "I have an appointment in thirty minutes. Thanks for the party, Laurel. Happy Birthday, Micah."

In less than an hour, no one was left in the garden except Laurel and Micah. Since many of her friends had hugged Laurel when they left and thanked her for the party, Micah put his arms around her and drew her close.

"What a nice thing to do for me," he murmured into the fragrance of her soft hair. "And what a great group of people. I've never enjoyed a birthday more. When I'm on assignment I lose track of the date, and sometimes my birthday comes and goes before I remember it. But I won't forget this one."

His strong arms around her gave Laurel such a sense of security that she would have been content to stay there forever. But she was in no position to start a romance. With the heavy suspense hanging over her, she couldn't think any further than Debbie's wedding.

Reluctantly, she slipped from his arms. "Let's sit down for a while and then you can help me carry things into the house. It's been fun, but I'm bushed, and I'll be glad for a little peace and quiet. Our congregation is a noisy bunch when they're having fun."

"But it's quite an experience for me to see the close fellowship you have. I'm beginning to realize what I've missed by worshiping in private. And the pastor's message this morning changed my life. I want you to be the first to know that after we came home from church, I accepted Jesus as my personal Savior."

This time Laurel initiated the hug as she put her arms around Micah's waist and stood on tiptoe to kiss his cheek. He pulled her into a closer embrace and tipped her chin. A tender smile hovered around his lips as he bent to her. Laurel made no attempt to avoid his seeking mouth, but lifted her face eagerly. The long kiss brought happiness too deep for words, but Laurel soon pulled away from him.

She'd made up her mind not long after Jason died that she wouldn't marry another person who didn't accept her faith. And in the past few days when she'd considered her growing feelings for Micah, she couldn't see any reason not to love him except the differences in their spiritual beliefs. That was no longer a problem.

Micah touched the soft curve of her cheek. "Should I apologize for being so impetuous?"

She shook her head, and he heard a soft sniffle.

"I'm fond of you, Laurel, or I wouldn't have kissed you. You haven't known me very long, but let me assure you that I'm not one of these guys who have a girl in every port."

"Please, Micah, let's not talk about it. I'll admit that I liked your kiss, or I wouldn't have responded like I did. But I've got a lot on my mind this summer."

She was somewhat disappointed when he said, "I

understand," and started picking up dishes to carry inside.

"You don't have to help this time. Today's your birthday. Look at your cards while I clear the table and put things in the dishwasher."

He was chuckling over Debbie's card when she returned to the garden. A large 50 covered the front of the card, and the inside caption read, "But who's counting?"

"I can't believe you and your friends would do all this for me," he said. "I'm embarrassed by so much attention."

"They're a wonderful church family. I couldn't have weathered my many crises without their support. There comes a time when you can't handle things alone."

He continued opening his birthday cards. He didn't recognize all of the names, but he was touched by the warm messages the cards conveyed. Laurel directed a smile toward him when he read the last card aloud. "The more you have the sweeter they are."

Believing that Laurel wanted to be alone, he stood up, saying, "Would you like for me to leave these cards so you can read them?" he said. "These total more cards than I've received in my previous fifty years."

"Yes, I'll read them before I go to bed."

"I've got a long trip planned for tomorrow, and I have some computer work to do."

Micah wanted the feel of Laurel in his arms, and he wondered if he'd be out of line to hug her again. Deciding it was worth a try, he took her hand and pulled her toward him. She came willingly, and holding her loosely in his arms, he said, "Thanks again. It's been a wonderful day."

Her lips were slightly parted as she leaned back in his arms and looked up at him. Although wanting to kiss that sensitive mouth again, with a sigh, he leaned forward and kissed her on the forehead. Micah's eyes caught and held hers for a long moment before he released her and left the garden. He couldn't promise Laurel anything yet, so he needed to curb his emotions.

Chapter Eight

Micah spent five days in New York, but he phoned Laurel each day to check on her. When she got up on Saturday morning, she saw that Micah had come home sometime in the night, and her pulse raced at the thought of seeing him again.

It had rained most of the week, and she hadn't been able to work outside. She'd spent her time refinishing the stair treads on the main staircase, and the house smelled of varnish and oils. She and Debbie had used the rear staircase to reach their rooms.

She wanted to put another coat on the stairs today, but when the grass dried, she'd have to start mowing. So much work to do, so little time to do it. And she was worried about her finances, too, because Pete had called this morning saying that the barn roof needed replacing because a large tree had fallen on it.

When Debbie came downstairs for breakfast and

found Laurel tallying up planned wedding expenses, she finally put her foot down and demanded that her mother forget about buying new draperies for the downstairs.

"Mom," Debbie said in exasperation. "We don't have the money to buy new draperies. Most of the wedding guests won't even be in the house, and besides, they've all seen the house like it is. I've never known you to be so reckless in spending money. Don't you know how guilty I feel that you're spending so much money for a one-day event?"

Tears welled in Laurel's eyes, and she buried her head on the table. "It's not a one-day event," she said. "You'll only have *one* first wedding day, and I want it to be one you will remember."

Debbie knelt by her mother's chair. "Mom, I *will* remember it. But I won't remember it with pleasure if you're left with a lot of bills to pay. And, please, don't buy that sterling silver flatware for our wedding gift. You've sacrificed for me all of my life. I appreciate that. It's the only gift I want from you. Please."

Laurel nodded, and for one of the few times in her life, she felt like unleashing her anger on Debbie. She got up from the table and went out on the porch to prepare to varnish. If she stayed any longer, she'd say things she'd regret.

"Mom," Debbie beseeched.

"Leave me alone, Debbie. You've made your point, and I'll do what you say. I won't discuss it anymore."

Debbie turned away with a bleak expression in her eyes and went upstairs, and Laurel was sorry for her attitude. But Debbie didn't seem to understand *her* position. How could she explain to Debbie the empty feeling that, after looking after her for twenty-two years, she would no longer be needed? Or how it saddened her that Debbie would be living in Colorado, and she'd only see her two or three times a year? Or how confining it was to be tied to Oaklawn, trying to maintain it for Debbie and her future children? Or how she dreaded the thought of being alone day after day?

Maybe she'd made a mistake by not defying her in-laws and moving out of their house and making a life of her own. Cousin Kevin had often told her that she wasn't being fair to herself or to Debbie by allowing Debbie's interests to monopolize her time. More than once, he'd said, "Sell Oaklawn and forget about your promise to Jason's parents. You devoted many years to them, and they should never have tried to control your future."

As Laurel carefully applied the final coat of finish to the broad stair treads, her anger cooled somewhat, and she supposed she would have to apologize to Debbie. Goodness knows, her daughter had never asked for much. Laurel had always anticipated Debbie's wishes and provided them.

Up until this moment, Laurel had believed that she was a strong-willed person. Now she wondered if she was weak—depending on others for her motivation in life. Was she always going to be a mirror reflecting the desires of others? Was it time for her to assert herself and do what *she* wanted for a change?

Conscience-stricken over such a selfish thought, she remembered the Bible taught the way to serve God was to serve others. Well, she'd done that, and received little thanks for it, she thought rebelliously. She'd been a dutiful daughter-in-law, caring for her husband's ailing parents as if they were her own. She'd tried to be both mother and father to Debbie. And she'd been active in the mission work of the local church. She couldn't regret doing what she had, but was it time for her to become reckless? Her response to Micah's caresses had convinced her that she could embrace a new life. After all, forty-two wasn't too old for many things—love included.

As her rebellious thoughts continued, she decided it was time for her to make a statement and change her old life. She was tired of red hair, and she daringly thought she might try a new color. She'd go to the beauty stop every week, instead of every few months when she needed a haircut. She'd start getting weekly manicures, maybe even have a pedicure. She wouldn't even rule out a monthly massage. The idea of doing what *she* wanted to do was becoming more and more appealing. Applying the varnish with swift, broad strokes, she was impulsively considering a *weekly* massage when her thoughts were interrupted by a knock at the porch door.

"Who is it?" she demanded.

"Micah."

"Just a minute," she said, and her good humor was restored instantly. She laid aside the brush and went to the door.

Micah was dressed in denim shorts and a sleeveless shirt that emphasized his muscular arms and shoulders.

"Good morning, ma'am," he said in a servile tone and touched an imaginary cap. "Beggin' your pardon, ma'am, but 'pears to me your grass needs cuttin'. Could you furnish a meal for a poor man in exchange for a day's work?"

Micah had quickly noticed Laurel's reddened eyes and her drooping lips. She brightened at his levity.

"The lady of the house can provide a meal in short order, but she's expecting to mow the grass herself this afternoon."

She unlatched the door, and he stepped inside. Sniffing, he said, "Painting something?"

"Refinishing the staircase. I've been at it all week. I'm going to keep working so the brush won't dry, but help yourself to a cup of coffee in the kitchen."

"No, thanks. I was joking. I just had a combined breakfast and lunch. I've had a rough week, so I slept late this morning. I'm serious about mowing the lawn. I'd enjoy it." He held out his hand. "Give me the key to the outbuilding. The grass is dry enough to start now."

She searched his eyes and knew he wanted to help

her. She was so unaccustomed to having people concerned about her that it was little wonder that she'd
been drawn to Micah right from the start.

"My hands are sticky, but you'll find the key hanging on a hook in the kitchen. It's labeled Garden House.
Thanks, Micah."

Laurel was busily stroking the steps with the brush
and humming a hymn when he returned from the
kitchen. She dimpled at him. "I'll have your meal ready
when you finish your work."

He shook his head. "I was joking about that. But I
do expect to be paid," he said in mock severity.

"How's that?"

"If I mow the grass for you, that should buy you
some extra time. I'm going to research another home
near Knoxville on Monday. I want you to go with me."

Laurel opened her mouth to refuse, but she suddenly
remembered her resolution to start living recklessly.

"I'll do it," she said, "but I'll still expect you for
supper."

"You've talked me into it."

As he turned toward the porch, she said, "By the way,
I'm going to dye my hair brown."

Micah's jaw dropped and he gasped. His response
amused her. "I take it you don't approve."

"If you dye your hair, I may have to turn you over
my knee…"

"You wouldn't dare!" she said, and her eyes glinted
dangerously. He dodged instinctively as the varnish

brush winged toward him, but he reached out a deft hand and caught it by the handle.

"How dare you throw a brush at me," he said as he struggled to control his laughter. "That was an idle threat intended to intimidate you, but I see it didn't work. I wouldn't dream of striking you, but why would you want to dye your hair?"

"I've decided to live recklessly."

"If you want to live recklessly, take a raft trip down the Grand Canyon or climb Mount Everest. Please don't dye your beautiful hair." He took a step toward her and handed her the brush. "I can't imagine you without red hair."

Ashamed of her sudden burst of temper and touched by the distress in his strong face, she said softly, "I promise I won't dye my hair. I'll find some other way to prove my independence."

He moved toward the door, and when he was a safe distance from the lethal varnish brush, he said, "On second thought, maybe you should change the color of your hair. I've always heard that red hair and temper are interlinked. If you have brown hair, it might be more peaceful around here."

He dodged out the door, but he heard her call, "Coward!" Micah grinned widely because he'd detected the sound of laughter in her voice.

They started at nine o'clock on Monday morning. As they drove through Knoxville, they saw Kevin entering his office. Micah tooted the horn. Kevin turned from the doorway and returned Laurel's wave.

"I didn't see him at church yesterday," Micah said.

"He left a week ago to visit one of his daughters in Florida. I didn't know he was home."

Micah's goal for the day was to research and photograph one of the oldest brick houses in western Tennessee. The house, now operated as a museum, had been built when the area was still endangered from Cherokee threats. It resembled a fort more than a dwelling. The outer walls, eighteen inches thick, had portholes, and the attic had windows designed to be used by sharpshooters. The near-flat roof originally had a lookout post. Massive double shutters were designed to protect the great windows in time of attack, and a place of refuge had been constructed in the cellars. For emergency escapes, there was a trapdoor on the second floor leading to a hidden closet at ground level, and an underground passage providing access to the barn.

Laurel stayed close to Micah as he took numerous photos on several different cameras. She didn't want to break his concentration, so she spoke very little as he made notes and took measurements of some features of the house. Laurel was naturally interested in seeing historic houses since she'd lived in one for so long. She welcomed a chance to see other old dwellings, especially when it provided an opportunity to spend the day with Micah. They left the old landmark at four o'clock.

"I'm hungry," Micah said. "That package of crackers and can of iced tea at lunch didn't satisfy my hunger. It's early, but let's stop at a restaurant."

They lingered long over their meal, enjoying being together, and it was almost eight o'clock when they got home.

"It's been a wonderful day," Laurel said as Micah turned off the highway into Oaklawn's driveway.

He laid his hand on her shoulder and squeezed it gently. "It's always a wonderful day when I'm with you," he said softly. "I—" He braked sharply, forgetting what he'd intended to say.

Laurel had lowered her lashes at his comment, but she looked up quickly when he stopped so abruptly. The sun hovered on the western horizon, and Laurel stared in stunned belief at the sight before them.

"What's happened?" she screamed.

Her home looked as if it had been trashed. Trees and shrubbery were draped with long, white streamers. As Micah put the car into motion again, Laurel saw that the streamers were strips of toilet paper. Dozens of rolls must have been used to achieve such a disastrous result.

Micah pointed to the east wall of the house. White graffiti had been sprayed in spirals from top to bottom. Although she'd been trying to control her temper lately, Laurel felt blood rushing to her face, and she pounded the dashboard of the car with her fists. Micah stopped the car and caught her hands in his. She struggled to free them, and he said quietly, but sternly, "Stop it! You're going to hurt yourself, to say nothing of damaging this rental car. Anger never does any good."

"It does me good," Laurel said. "I've never been so mad in my life. If I can find out who did this, I'll have them arrested. I'll never get all of this paper picked up before the wind scatters it from here to Virginia. And I suppose that graffiti will be permanent." She tugged to free her hands, and Micah let her go.

She jumped out of the car and slammed the door. She looked around wildly, and fearing that she would harm herself, Micah moved quickly to her side. He didn't know what to do. She obviously wasn't in the mood to be told to calm down, so he said nothing, but he watched her closely. Laurel walked back and forth in the driveway, weaving from one side to the other, occasionally kicking a piece of limestone that got in her way.

He understood her anger. He was angry, too, that someone was trying to thwart her efforts to make a showplace out of Oaklawn. He held a proprietary attitude toward Laurel, and he resented anything that caused trouble for her. While he kept one eye on Laurel, Micah looked for clues to determine when the vandalism had taken place.

Laurel must have been walking with her eyes closed, and he ran toward her when she tumbled headlong into a large spruce tree whose branches spread over the ground. She disappeared from sight beneath the massive foliage. All he could see of Laurel were her red shoes. Grinning, he hurried over to her, figuring that his help wouldn't be appreciated, but he had to find out if she was injured.

He heard her pounding the ground in frustration like a child having a tantrum. He knelt on the ground and separated the branches just as she ceased her struggling. She was lying face down in a carpet of spruce needles, but he heard the faint hint of a sniffle.

"Are you hurt?" he said softly.

The red head shook negatively.

"Come on out and let me see. You probably have some scratches."

"My own fault," she said tearfully.

Micah took hold of her shoe and tugged. "Come on. I've been looking around. The damage isn't as bad as you think. We can get this cleaned up in a few hours."

He tugged on her foot again, and her flare of temper disappeared as quickly as it had come. Micah was right—anger never did any good, and she was ashamed of her actions.

"Go away, please!" she begged, and he knew she had calmed down. "I'm not fit company for anyone now."

He took hold of her shoes and pulled. Kicking her feet free from his grasp, Laurel turned over on her back, sat up and scooted out from under the tree. She sat with downcast eyes.

Dried spruce needles stuck out of her red hair, and her head resembled a porcupine's back. Her face was dirty, and there was a long scratch marring the smooth perfection of her complexion. Her lips pursed in an endearing pout. She could easily have been a ten year old instead of a woman in her mellow years.

"Go away," she said again.

Striving to hide his amusement, Micah lifted her chin, and she closed her eyes, refusing to meet his gaze.

"Are you going to say, 'I told you so?'" she asked.

"No."

She opened her eyes, and Micah's smile was alive with affection. She bit her lip, but he knew her anger had lessened.

"Help me up," she demanded, "and take that smile off of your face."

He took her hand and lifted her to her feet. She stumbled a little.

"Did you hurt yourself?" he asked quickly.

"I skinned my knees. But I have no one to blame except myself. You're right, anger never does any good."

He took his handkerchief and tenderly wiped the grime from her face, carefully dabbing at the long scratch. "You have needles stuck in your hair." He threaded his long fingers through her curls and removed the offending needles.

With her anger spent, Laurel succumbed to exhaustion, and she sat on a bench and stared at her vandalized home and landscape.

"I'll never get that graffiti off the wall."

"I'm not so sure. It's not paint, but some kind of cream, probably shaving cream, sprayed from a pressurized can. It's already fading somewhat, but I can hose it down, and there won't be any residue left at all."

"I wonder if this was done after Debbie left for work?"

"She would have left you a note if she'd seen the vandalism. Why not check in the house and see if there's a message from her?"

"Okay, but I hope she didn't see it."

"Be sure and wash your face and put ointment on that scratch," he advised. "You don't want to get an infection. Is your hose in the garden house?"

She nodded.

"If you'll hand out the key, I'll get the hose and start washing down the brick wall."

"Thank you. I'll pick up the paper. I hope we can get it cleared before dark. I don't want Debbie to be startled when she drives in."

"Maybe it's time to call the police," Micah said.

Laurel shook her head, a stubborn expression on her face. "I don't want Debbie to know. Also, if the scattered Cooper family hears about it, some of them would insist on putting in their two cents' worth about what I should do."

"Even Cousin Kevin?" Micah inquired, a humorous quirk around his mouth.

"Especially Cousin Kevin," Laurel said. "He's been a big help to me in many ways, but sometimes he annoys me." She hadn't told Micah about Kevin's proposal, and she doubted that she ever would.

Debbie hadn't left a message, so the vandalism had occurred after four o'clock. If she and Micah had come on home instead of stopping for dinner, they might have caught the culprit. She cleansed and treated her face, but she kept on her dirty clothes, because she knew she'd need to shower after she cleaned up the paper.

Micah had already cleaned a portion of the wall when Laurel went out. "It's cleaning right off," Micah assured her, but she winced when she saw the soapy water that covered the shrubbery and flowers beside the house. Quick to notice anything that concerned Laurel, Micah put his hand over the nozzle and stopped the flow of water.

"What is it?"

"That cream might ruin my plants, but there's no other way to get the wall cleaned."

"Shall I continue then?"

"Yes, of course," she said, but she thought of all the money she'd spent landscaping Oaklawn, some of it now being washed away. Despite Debbie's accusation, she didn't consider herself a spendthrift. She'd never had enough money to be a big spender, but since it seemed she was always short of money, she apparently was spending above her means.

Her thoughts were heavy as she gathered armfuls of paper from the lawn. She didn't know of anyone who hated her, so the only explanation must be that someone wanted to scare her away from Oaklawn. As discouraged as she was now, she was tempted to call Cousin Kevin and tell him to sell the property.

Darkness had fallen by the time Micah finished spraying the shaving cream from the house. He washed most of the muck off the plants, having no idea whether the water that soaked into the ground would destroy the flowers and shrubs. As soon as he put the hose away, he went to help Laurel. She already had two large garbage bags stuffed full of paper. The two security lights illuminated the lawn well enough that the rest of the paper was easy to find. They didn't finish until after ten o'clock.

"At least we finished before Debbie came home," Laurel said, as they walked toward the house, carrying the bags.

"Are you as tired as I am?" she asked.

"Not knowing how tired you are, I can't answer that," Micah teased. But he knew she was worn out because she walked as if every step was an effort. "But in spite of all this, I enjoyed our day together."

"Yes. So did I. If I have trouble going to sleep tonight, I'll think of the nice things we did. And I'm glad that I didn't have to face this latest fiasco alone." She stopped at the mailbox beside the driveway and drew out a packet of mail.

"Thanks for everything," she said as they deposited the garbage bags in the Dumpster. "And I'm sorry I threw such a tantrum. I haven't done anything like that in years."

He put his arm around her, and in spite of the weariness of her body, she leaned into his embrace and his arms tightened. She'd never known tenderness from any man like Micah had shown her. She wouldn't name her feelings for him, but she'd become very fond of him this summer, and she knew that when he left Oaklawn, he would leave a void in her life. She dreaded the thought of winter approaching without either Debbie or Micah. She wondered if out of sheer loneliness she would accept Cousin Kevin's offer. He had everything to offer her—except love.

She went inside and leafed through the mail before she went upstairs to a shower and hopefully a good night's sleep. The envelope without a return address alerted her, and she turned the white envelope over and over. No clue to whom the sender might be.

She was tempted to throw it into the trash can without opening it, but curiosity stimulated her courage. A single white page was in the envelope. She spread out the paper.

Ye shall be brought to the grave. Job 21:32.

The letter had been mailed in Chattanooga.

Chapter Nine

Laurel shed tears of frustration as she hurried upstairs to hide the envelope. Her wonderful day with Micah had been spoiled by the way it had ended. The vandalism had been almost more than she could bear, and now this letter. Hearing Debbie's car on the limestone driveway, she quickly turned off the light. Until she could compose herself, she couldn't talk to Debbie.

She kicked off her shoes, lay on the bed and pulled on a blanket, hoping that her daughter wouldn't stop for a chat. Debbie's steps sounded on the stairway. The door to Laurel's room opened a crack, and she didn't stir. She could hear Debbie wait a few moments, close the door and go to her room.

Quietly, Laurel got up and removed her clothes, flung them across a chair and put on the nightgown she'd brought from the bathroom. She was too tired to take the dirty clothes to the hamper.

This summer that she'd expected to be a time of joy for Debbie and her was turning into a nightmare. If Micah hadn't come to Oaklawn, she believed she might have collapsed with all of the stress and worry she'd suffered. Had God sent Micah at this particular time when she needed so much help and encouragement? She sensed that Micah's feelings for her transcended mere friendship. Was it God's will for them to marry?

Now that Micah had accepted Jesus as his Savior, he had all the qualities that she could ever want in a husband. And it seemed ironic now that, as Micah's spiritual enlightenment increased, her personal faith was at low ebb. She'd been as devout a Christian as she'd known how to be. Her greatest desire had been to have God's will fulfilled in her life. Why, then, was He putting her through this time of testing? Near the breaking point, she cried out, as Jesus had done on the cross, the words of the psalmist David, "My God, my God, why have you forsaken me?"

She knew her lack of faith was displeasing to God, and if Micah knew how her faith was faltering, it would be a detriment to his new walk in the Lord. She would tell Micah about this letter because she'd promised, but she couldn't talk to him about her lack of faith.

"God," she murmured, "is there no end to the things I have to keep to myself. I can't let Micah see how much I doubt Your providence."

Laurel did sleep for a few hours, but she woke at her usual time. The phone rang while she was in the shower.

She hurriedly wrapped a large beach towel around her and went to answer. Not until she had her hand on the phone did she wonder if this was her tormentor. Her relief was intense when she heard Micah's voice.

"How did you sleep?" he asked.

"Poorly."

"I was afraid of that. I didn't sleep much, either—I kept wondering who's harassing you and why."

"I had another letter in yesterday's mail."

"So that's the reason you couldn't sleep." In a protective tone she liked, he said, "Why didn't you call me?"

"You couldn't have done anything."

"I've been thinking that it might be a good idea not to tell anyone what we found when we came home last night."

Micah was a bit surprised at his words. When had he started thinking of Oaklawn as home?

"Not even Debbie?"

"It would only upset her. If we say nothing, the responsible person might wonder why and make some comment that would alert you to whoever is behind all of these things."

"Yes. You're right. And since there's only another month until the wedding, I don't want Debbie to be worried. If she knows what's going on, she'll be even more disturbed about leaving me."

Following the pattern of previous harassment, several days passed without any calls or intimidating letters. But when the phone rang at two o'clock in the morning almost a week after the vandalism, Laurel was afraid to answer. But a desperate need to identify her tormentor gave her the courage to lift the receiver. Holding her breath, she said nothing.

"This is Micah."

Her sense of relief was so great she almost dropped the receiver. "Oh, my! You nearly scared the wits out of me."

"Sorry, but there are a couple of cows on the lawn. It's been raining all night and the ground is mushy. If these cows keep running around, they'll ruin the grass. We'd better do something about it."

"Oh, my!" she said again. "I'll meet you downstairs."

She threw off her nightgown, reached into the clothes hamper and retrieved the jeans and shirt she'd worn yesterday. She grabbed a flashlight from the dresser top.

She heard cows bawling the minute she stepped out on the back porch where Micah waited for her. They walked around the lawn to investigate, but it was pitch-dark when they got away from the security lights.

"You say there are two cows?"

"I saw two at one time, but there may be more. They're white cows—Charolais, I think."

"Pete is pasturing some Charolais cattle in one of Oaklawn's fields. I'll call him."

She flashed her light on the dark lawn and saw that the cattle's hooves had sunk deep into the thick turf she'd been nurturing all summer. A cow came around the corner of the house and plodded through her petunia bed. Angrily, Laurel turned toward the house, praying for the strength to control her tongue.

"Pete," she said when her neighbor sleepily answered the phone. "Your cows are out, and they're trampling my lawn and flower beds."

She heard him yawn. "All of them?"

"All of them what?"

"Is the whole herd out?"

"How would I know? It's dark outside. We've only seen two or three."

"I'm sorry, Laurel. I'll come right away."

When she rejoined Micah, she said, "It will take Pete a little while to get here. Come in the kitchen, and I'll make some tea."

She set two cups of water in the microwave to heat and put a basket filled with tea bags of different blends on the table. When the water was ready, she gave a cup to Micah and sat opposite him.

"Laurel," Micah asked thoughtfully. "How do you get along with your neighbor? Could he be the one harassing you? Since his property adjoins yours, seems to me he'd be the most likely person to want to buy your place. How well do you know him?"

"Pete and his wife are in their fifties, and we've been friends since I moved here. Their daughter, Kaitlyn, will be Debbie's maid of honor. They go to church with me. In fact, they attended your birthday bash. He's the tall, gangly man who looks like he's starving to death, but can put away more food in one meal than you'd eat in a day. I'd have to catch him in the act to believe he'd do anything like that mess we had when we returned from Knoxville last week."

"Well, it was just a thought," Micah said as he dangled a tea bag in the mug of hot water.

Laurel looked haggard, and he knew these incidents were taking a toll on her. She was a strong woman, but he feared if she didn't get some relief from these annoying incidents, she'd collapse as soon as Debbie's wedding was over.

Her hand drummed nervously on the tabletop, and he covered her hand with his. "Occasionally, I wonder if these things are happening, or if I'm losing my mind."

"Don't forget I saw the vandalism a few nights ago," Micah assured her. "It's happening, all right."

A vehicle pulled into the driveway. Micah took a large swallow of tea, set the cup on the table and followed Laurel into the yard.

Brenda Howe was driving the pickup. "I'm really sorry about this, Laurel," she said, and Micah recognized her as one of the women from Bethel Church. "I hope there isn't much damage. Pete is checking the pasture, and he'll join us soon."

"He won't be able to see much until daylight comes," Laurel said.

When Pete walked around the house fifteen minutes later, his face was grave. "I hate to say this, but I think someone cut the fence and drove the cattle onto your lawn, but I can tell better as soon as it's light." He took off his cap and ran nervous fingers through his thick crop of gray hair. "How long have the cattle been out?"

Laurel looked toward Micah, who stood in the background. "Micah heard them and called me."

"I sleep with my window open," Micah said, "and I'm a light sleeper. I suppose the cattle running by my window woke me, but I didn't realize what it was until I heard the cows bawling. I didn't actually see them on the lawn until I called Laurel about two o'clock. They're doing a lot of damage. I'll help round them up now, if you want to try."

"I'll go, too," Laurel said.

"Okay," Pete said. "I've got some extra lights in the truck."

"I'll leave a note on the kitchen table for Debbie, in case she misses us," Laurel said. "But she's always so tired when she comes home from work, she sleeps like a log for several hours."

Although there was a possibility that some of the cows had bypassed the house and were in the wooded area toward the highway, Pete figured they wouldn't have left the lush grass to graze in the forest. So the four of them fanned out over the lawn and moved steadily toward the pasture. One cow with a calf beside her resisted all of Laurel's efforts to shoo her toward the enclosure. She'd apparently had a taste of freedom and liked it.

Once Laurel's feet skidded out from under her and she landed on her fanny. The rain had slowed to a drizzle, but she was wet and miserable by the time she prodded the cow and calf into the pasture enclosure. The Howes and Micah were there ahead of Laurel, and when Pete closed the gate behind the two animals Laurel had found, he said, "That's all of them. I only had fourteen head of cattle in this field."

While Pete patched the fence to keep the cattle inside, he and Micah agreed that the wire had been cut.

"But I don't understand it," Pete said. "This goes beyond some childish prank. Were they picking on you or me, Laurel?"

Too weary to speak, she shrugged.

"I have a buyer coming for these cattle day after tomorrow. I need the money to pay off a note at the bank. It would have been rough for me to lose the cattle at this time. But I don't know why that's important to someone else."

"Somebody might be trying to mess up Oaklawn so it won't be nice for Debbie's wedding," Brenda said. "A few people in the area think Debbie should have married a local man, rather than an out-of-state guy she'd met at a national church seminar she'd attended two years ago in D.C."

Laurel knew the vandalism was aimed at her, but since she didn't know the reason, she said nothing.

Daylight came slowly as they walked back to the house. The lawn was in a sorry mess. Each step the cows made had left an indentation, and not only were the petunias ruined, but also a bed of hostas. Fortunately, the animals hadn't broken through the fence into the rose garden.

"I'll make good on the damages, Laurel," Pete said. "Have everything repaired and send me the bill. I think my insurance will cover this."

Too disheartened at the moment to really care what happened, she said wearily, "I'll have to think about what I can do, but I'll keep the expense as low as possible."

For the next week, a landscaper worked, filling in the holes, planting grass seed and replacing the damaged petunias and hostas. Dozens of the neighbors stopped by to see the damage and offered to help, but Laurel thanked them and told them she had hired a professional to do the work. The landscaper was almost finished when Cousin Kevin came. He didn't know about the damage to Laurel's lawn until he drove in and saw the workers.

"What's going on?" he said when Laurel went out on the portico to greet him. They sat in two of the rockers while she explained briefly.

"Pete needs to keep a closer rein on his livestock. He's going to pay for this damage, I take it."

"He said he would, but I don't know that I'll accept it. It wasn't his fault."

"It's his place to keep his cattle restricted. I still think you should have a written contract with him."

This had been a point of contention between Laurel and Kevin. He hadn't approved when she'd rented the farm to Pete and Brenda. Her anger kindled at his aggressive attitude, and she didn't tell him that the fence had been cut.

The next day Debbie and Laurel spent several hours in Knoxville making last-minute wedding preparations. When they returned, she saw a muddy footprint on the porch, and inside the house there was a scent she couldn't identify. The exotic smell permeated the house, and she had the distinct feeling that someone had been inside. It couldn't have been Micah, because he'd been gone all day.

Debbie apparently didn't notice anything unusual, so Laurel didn't mention her suspicions.

After dinner, Debbie went to spend the night with Kaitlyn Howe, so they could prepare bags of birdseed for the wedding guests to throw at the bridal couple. When Laurel was ill at ease as she was tonight, she could calm her nerves by cooking or baking. She'd gotten a basket of peaches at the market this afternoon, and they were just ripe enough to make freezer jam. As she peeled and quartered the peaches before she ground them in the food processor, she made an effort not to think how much she and Debbie enjoyed this succulent jam on ice cream, biscuits and pancakes. She faced a traumatic change in her lifestyle, and she intended to react with a smile on her face, even if she was crying inside. When the jam was prepared, she poured it into pint-size plastic containers, covered them and left them on the kitchen cabinet until the next day when she would put the jam in the freezer.

By the time she finished, Laurel had been on her feet several hours, and she was tired, but remembering the feeling that someone had been in the house, she looked through every room before she went to bed. Finding everything in order, she went to sleep immediately.

When she woke she was sitting up in bed with the quilt close around her. It seemed as if she'd heard someone talking. Had Debbie and Kaitlyn decided to spend the night at Oaklawn?

"Hello, Laurel," a muffled male voice said. The unfamiliar voice chanted in a monotone, "Death is only a dream."

The phone receiver was still in place. Her pulse beating erratically, Laurel looked around wildly. Was someone in the room with her? Had someone come in earlier today and stayed in the house?

"Goodbye," the voice said, and a chilly, tense silence filled the room.

Laurel jumped out of bed, shrugged into her terrycloth robe and buttoned it as she ran downstairs. She was halfway across the lawn to Micah's apartment, screaming out his name when it dawned on her that she was barefoot. She had reached the top of the steps, ready to pound on his door when she came to a sudden stop. What would Micah think of her coming to his door in her night clothes?

She hoped he'd understand, because she had to have help. Before she could knock on the door, she heard his footsteps in the room. Clad in his pajamas, his hair ruffled, his eyes heavy with sleep, Micah opened the door. Obviously, he'd been sound asleep, but had wakened instantly at her screams.

She pushed past him into the room, and he hurriedly grabbed a robe from the closet and put it on before he went to her.

"My love, what's happened?" he said, the word of endearment slipping out, but she seemed not to notice.

She stepped close to him. Her teeth chattered. The night was hot and humid, so she wasn't cold, but she was terribly frightened. He pulled her into his arms, and she wrapped her arms around his waist.

"I can't take it anymore. I don't know if I can ever go back in that house again."

She looked up at him piteously, and her lips trembled. The tears in her green eyes reminded him of the ocean, and knowing of no better way to comfort her, he leaned forward and kissed her. Laurel stiffened at first, then she yielded herself to his embrace and returned his kiss. Micah felt like he'd been hit by a bolt of lightning, and he kissed her again.

Feeling as if she was forsaking light for darkness, Laurel gently pushed him away, eluding his seeking arms.

Chapter Ten

"I think somebody is in the house," she said. "I woke up and a man was talking to me. It sounded as if he was in the room."

"Was he?"

"I don't know. I didn't see anybody, but I didn't stay to find out. I ran downstairs and came over here. When I came home from town this afternoon, I sensed somebody had been in the house, but before I went to bed, I looked around and didn't see anyone. And nothing looked out of place."

"Debbie?"

"She's spending the night with Kaitlyn."

"What did you hear?"

"I was so scared, I can't remember for sure, but I think someone said, 'Hello, Laurel.' He sang a few lines that said something about death being a dream. Then he said goodbye."

"I'll change out of my pajamas and go with you to check out the house. But I'm not a detective. I think it's time you talked to the police."

She shook her head. "No, it would ruin everything for Debbie. I've put up with it this long, I can manage another week."

If somebody killed her mother, Debbie's wedding would be ruined anyway, he thought. "Give me a few minutes to change, and we'll see what we can find."

He went into the bedroom and hurriedly put on shorts and a shirt, his mind rioting. He buckled on a pair of sandals. That kiss had proven that he did love Laurel. He'd lived fifty years without more than a passing interest in women, but Laurel had changed that. What kind of marriage could he anticipate when he was well into middle age? But he had to put his latent romantic feelings aside for the time being.

His immediate task was to see if there was anybody in Laurel's house, and to find out who was harassing her. But everything was on hold until after Debbie's wedding, since that was of primary interest to Laurel at the moment.

When he came from the bedroom, Laurel was leaning on the breakfast bar, her head pillowed in her arms. He wondered if she was asleep, but she stirred and stood wearily.

"Why don't you stay in the apartment and lock the door while I search? You can lie on the couch and rest."

"That's nice of you, but I'm going with you. I feel

mean enough to involve you in my difficulties—I can't let you search alone. I wouldn't have bothered you, but I was scared witless."

He put his arms around her shoulders. "I've told you to call if you needed me. You're a brave woman, but you can't carry the weight of the world on your shoulders."

As they went downstairs, she said wearily, "That's the way I've been feeling for years. I don't mean to complain, because God has supplied every need I've had. And I should have trusted Him to find the way out of this predicament rather than to have bothered you."

"The pastor said last Sunday that God uses people to accomplish His will. I'm happy I came to Oaklawn so I can help you."

She squeezed his hand. "So am I."

As they walked from the apartment to the porch, he asked, "Didn't you turn on any lights?"

She laughed slightly, ashamed of how she'd panicked. "If you'd seen how I bolted out of bed and ran downstairs, you'd know I wouldn't have had time to turn on any lights. I had a flashlight, and with the security lights, I could see well enough. In case you do decide this is a matter for the cops, let's wear gloves so we won't contaminate the evidence."

Laurel got a package of "one-size-fits-all" gloves she'd bought for yard use from a cabinet on the back porch, put on a pair and handed another pair to Micah.

Turning on all the lights as they went, they started in the basement and covered every room, and by the time they reached the attic, Micah was convinced there wasn't anyone in the house. Nearing exhaustion, Laurel sat on the narrow flight of stairs while Micah checked the attic.

He sat beside her when he came back, and their shoulders touched. "There's no one in this house, but the house may be bugged some way. Let's look in your bedroom for a hidden microphone."

They looked in the dresser drawers and the closets without finding anything. But when Micah crawled under the bed, using a flashlight, he found a small tape recorder, apparently activated by a timer. He sat on the floor by the bed and pushed Rewind and Play, but there wasn't any message. Apparently, the device was set to erase as it played.

"Whoever planned this is pretty clever and knows how to cover his tracks. Why don't you put this with the other things you've collected this summer? It might be used as evidence if you ever have to prove what's been happening."

She showed him the letters she'd received and put the tape recorder in the box with them.

"Thanks for helping tonight," she said. "Go on back to your apartment and get some rest." She took a blanket from the linen closet. "I'm going to sleep on the couch the rest of the night. I know I won't go to sleep in here."

Laurel detained Micah a moment longer at the foot of the steps to find out something that concerned her.

"I know your research work is about finished. When will you leave, Micah?"

"My research is finished, and I'm already working on my article. But your trouble is my trouble. I won't leave until you have this situation resolved. I can write the article here as well as anywhere."

His words reassured Laurel, but she didn't expect Micah to neglect his work.

"Besides, there's something I haven't told you. I've been invited to join the staff of Walden College. I've hesitated to tell you until I'd made a decision."

Her eyes brightened with pleasure. "Then you might stay here permanently?"

"The word 'permanent' scares me! I've been moving around the world for a long time, and I don't know if I'd be happy to stay anywhere all the time. I've enjoyed being here in this quiet atmosphere this summer, but will I eventually get bored? I've taught many college seminars, which I enjoyed, but never more than three weeks at a time. I won't agree to more than a part-time professorship to see how I like it. There's a book I want to write, and I might combine the two things."

Laurel experienced the first ray of hope she'd had since Debbie had told her she'd be moving to Colorado. She'd gotten so accustomed to having Micah next door that she dreaded his leaving almost as much as she did Debbie's. As the days had passed, especially with all the bad things happening at Oaklawn, Laurel doubted that she could ever stay here alone. More than once she'd considered selling the property and wondered if Cousin Kevin might want to buy it. She wouldn't sell it to anyone else without giving him the opportunity to buy, because his ancestors had lived there, too. But when she remembered his atrocious proposal, just to get hold of Oaklawn, he probably wouldn't take the property unless she went with it.

Micah watched the play of emotions on Laurel's face, trying to decide how she felt about his staying in the area.

"If I decide to stay, may I continue living in the apartment or do you have it promised to someone else?"

"It isn't promised. I've had inquiries but I haven't rented it yet."

"I'll make up my mind soon. I don't want to keep you from having a renter."

After her first joyous response to his announcement, Laurel hadn't looked his way. He gently touched her chin and turned her face toward him.

"By the expression on your face a few minutes ago, I gather that you wouldn't be displeased if I decide to stay. Am I right in thinking that? Or am I just another tenant to you?"

Her lashes drooped until he couldn't see her eyes. "You know better than that. I don't know how I would have survived this summer if you hadn't been nearby."

"But I don't want to be considered a safety valve— someone who's handy to have around in an emergency.

I need to know if you harbor any deeper emotions for me?"

Her lashes lifted, green eyes connecting with his blue eyes, and a rosy hue tinted her cheeks. She suddenly realized that the emotion she felt for Micah was more than mere friendship. Almost in a whisper, she said, "I have deeper feelings for you than I've ever experienced before. But with this mystery hanging over me, you can understand why I don't feel ready to explore those feelings."

Disregarding her last statement, he persisted. "Then you'd be pleased if I decide to stay in Tennessee?"

"Yes," she said quietly, but the simplicity of her reply was all the affirmation he needed. There was a future for him with Laurel if he decided to stay in Tennessee. But would her feelings change if he wanted to live elsewhere?

The long-awaited wedding day had finally come— one that Debbie had excitedly anticipated with pleasure, but one that Laurel had dreaded for months. As she lay in bed waiting for daylight, Laurel gave a last-minute mental check to see if everything was ready.

She'd heard nothing from her tormentor since the night she'd been scared and had run to Micah. Considering the emotional toll Debbie's marriage was taking on her, Laurel would be glad when the wedding was over. That way she wouldn't have to dread it anymore.

The rehearsal had been held at five o'clock the

night before. Several members of Dereck's family had come from Colorado, and his parents had hosted a rehearsal dinner at a four-star restaurant in Knoxville. Cousin Kevin acted as Laurel's escort to the dinner. Debbie also had asked him to sit beside Laurel at the wedding, because she thought Laurel would look lonely sitting by herself. Micah took pictures at the rehearsal, but he declined an invitation to the dinner that followed.

Laurel got up and looked out the window, and through the mist-shrouded morning, she saw the reception area. A meteorologist on a Knoxville TV station had predicted that the day would be clear and hot. Laurel could put up with the heat as long as it didn't rain. The tents were in place, and the workers were coming at nine o'clock to set up the chairs and tables. The florist would be there at the same time, as would the caterer to assemble the cake. After that, someone would have to be on guard all the time to prevent accidents.

She wasn't as sad as she'd expected to be, and Laurel wondered how much Micah's interest in her, and the promises she'd read in his eyes, had contributed to this attitude. But Laurel believed she'd arrived at the point where she could have a fulfilled life regardless of the circumstances. She'd already asked God to forgive the doubts about His love for her that she'd experienced a few weeks ago. Although she couldn't see why now, she was convinced that in the future she'd realize that there was a reason for the trials she'd endured this summer.

If nothing more, this time of doubt and testing had caused her faith to be stronger than it had ever been.

Debbie and Laurel had chosen to have their last breakfast by themselves and, having come to grips with Debbie's leaving, Laurel met her daughter with a smile when she came into the kitchen.

"God has sent us a beautiful day," she said. "I'll admit I had some doubts about planning an outdoor reception, but it's going to be perfect."

"It was good of Pete and Brenda to volunteer to watch over the cake and punch while we dress for the wedding. By that time the ladies from the church will be arriving with the food," Debbie said.

"We have very good neighbors."

"I'm glad. That way, I won't worry about you so much. Mom, I hate to leave you." Tears formed in Debbie's eyes, and Laurel struggled momentarily with her own emotions.

She hugged Debbie and said, "I know you do, and I hate to have you move so far away. But think of all the fun and anticipation when you come home for a visit."

"Or when you come to visit us."

"And there's always the telephone. We can talk often."

"Would you want to move to Colorado?"

"Not at this time in my life. In his type of work, Dereck may move several times, so I can't be following you around. It's the biblical way for man and wife to be on their own. The Scriptures teach that a man should leave his father and mother and be joined to his wife. That means the wife, too, must leave her family to be with her husband. I'll be fine. I've come to peace with your leaving."

"Thanks, Mom. You've taken a load off my mind. I've been feeling guilty about going away."

"Don't worry about it. Dereck is a fine man, and I like his family, too. You'll be in good hands in Colorado. I want you to be happy."

"Like you and Daddy were? You've never talked about him and your life together."

With a composed smile, Laurel said, "After twenty years it's hard to recall many things, but I do remember we were happy on our wedding day."

That answer seemed to satisfy Debbie, and Laurel was glad she'd suppressed Jason's true character. She didn't want anything to spoil Debbie's big day.

Chapter Eleven

The tones of the antique piano filled the house as the pianist from Bethel Church presented traditional and contemporary music for twenty minutes prior to the wedding ceremony. About thirty people were seated in the entrance hall, including Cousin Kevin's two daughters and their families, as well as some distant Cooper cousins. Watching them, Micah sensed that some of the men had more than a passing interest as they looked at the mansion, making him wonder if one of them was trying to force Laurel to sell her home.

Seemingly uncomfortable in a formal black robe, Pastor Jensen took his place at the foot of the stairs. Dereck and his brother, dressed in identical black three-button suits with pale gray accessories, walked slowly to the left of the minister. Dereck's three-year-old nephew, the ring bearer, also wore a black suit. He clutched the leg of his father's trousers and peered anxiously around the entrance hall, obviously looking for his mother.

Kaitlyn Howe, Debbie's maid of honor, wore a sleeve-less three-quarter-length dress of cream chiffon over mint green lining with ruffle detail at neckline and hem. She walked down the stairway and took her place to the left of the minister. The ring bearer's dainty five-year-old sister followed Kaitlyn, intently scattering rose petals.

The music swelled to a loud crescendo, and the pianist's fingers tapped a staccato warning before the room reverberated to the music of the Bridal Chorus from *Lohengrin*.

Debbie and Laurel appeared at the top of the stairs, paused momentarily, and slowly descended.

Debbie had chosen a lightly pearled white lace gown with off-the-shoulder neckline and long illusion sleeves with button detail and a chapel train. Instead of a veil, she wore a delicate crystal and rhinestone tiara.

Laurel, looking as lovely as her daughter, was dressed in a champagne, heavily beaded chiffon cap-sleeved A-line gown with a sweetheart neckline.

Micah took photos until they paused in front of the minister, and since there would be no more pictures until the conclusion of the vows, he took time to admire the woman he loved. He knew the bride should be the focal point at a wedding, but he couldn't take his eyes off of Laurel. Debbie was pretty, but she'd never have the beauty of her mother. And when he considered all of the trials that Laurel had endured, he wondered how she could have turned out as she had. It had to be an inner beauty spawned by her Christian faith.

While the minister spoke to Debbie and Dereck of the spiritual responsibilities of marriage, Micah renewed his conversion. Believing that Jesus was His Savior as well as his Lord, Micah knew that he was now in a condition to join his life with Laurel's. She had never said so outright, but he didn't believe she would marry anyone who didn't cherish the same spiritual values she did. He had made up his mind that he'd accept a part-time professorship at Walden College, and he intended to join the fellowship of Bethel Church.

Micah roused himself quickly from his roller-coaster emotions when the minister said, "You may now kiss the bride."

Debbie would never forgive him if he'd missed that event, and he snapped into action. If Debbie was going to be his daughter, he wanted to stay in her good graces. He put Laurel out of his mind and concentrated on photographing the rest of the wedding and the reception.

The bride and groom greeted everyone at the reception and participated in the customary rituals of cutting the cake and drinking glasses of punch with arms intertwined. After the bridal party ate a light dinner, Laurel and Kaitlyn went upstairs with Debbie to help her out of the wedding dress and into traveling clothes for the planned honeymoon to Niagara Falls. From New York, they would go directly to Colorado without returning to Oaklawn.

Debbie's room already looked empty. She'd packed all of her possessions in boxes that were stored in the U-Haul trailer, which Dereck's parents would tow to Colorado. She wouldn't return to Oaklawn until Thanksgiving or Christmas.

So far, Laurel hadn't shed any tears. She'd kept a smile on her face, sometimes with an effort, but now was the time she had to be bravest.

Exhilarated over the attention she'd received, Debbie had laughed and cried alternately through the afternoon. But she looked radiant now, as all brides should, when she turned to Laurel.

"Oh, Mom, I don't know what to say."

"Don't say anything. It's been a wonderful day, and I'm happy for you and Dereck. Today has been the culmination of my plans for you. Nothing will ever break the ties between us, but from now on, your priority should be Dereck and the grandkids I hope you have for me. I'll be fine."

But Debbie must not have been convinced that Laurel was doing as well as she pretended because when she said goodbye to Micah, embracing him and kissing his cheek, she whispered, "Look after Mom while you're here, will you?"

Micah gave her a thumbs-up and said softly, "I intend to."

As Debbie waved goodbye to everyone, and Dereck held the car door open for her, Micah momentarily wondered why she'd asked him instead of her cousin Kevin to look after her mother. Did Debbie suspect that there was more between Laurel and him than friendship? If so, she must approve.

Perhaps knowing that this was a difficult time for Laurel, as soon as the honeymoon car decorated with streamers and tin cans disappeared down the driveway, her church family rallied around her. "Now tell us what needs to be done," Pastor Jensen said.

"Goodness! I hardly know where to begin," Laurel said, looking around the lawn. "The rental company will be here within the hour, and they'll dismantle the tents and take the chairs. I'd like to send the leftover cake and the food to some of our shut-ins. Also, the top layer of the cake needs to be put in the freezer so Debbie and Dereck can have it on their first anniversary."

"I'll take care of the cake," Brenda Howe volunteered. "And a few of us will make up trays of food to take to the nursing homes."

"Could someone rearrange the flowers to be used in church on Sunday morning?" Laurel asked, and she soon had a volunteer for that.

Micah asked Johnny Sizemore, one of Laurel's renters who had returned for the wedding and had settled into his apartment next door to Micah's, to help him. They supervised restoring the staircase and the entrance hall to their normal condition, taking down all the decorations. Kaitlyn ran the sweeper in Debbie's bedroom. Within three hours, the guests were gone, and it was hard to believe that there had been a wedding. The lawn was ruffled where the guests had milled around, but a few days of growth would take care of that.

Suddenly Laurel was alone.

Micah had taken his film into Knoxville to send it for processing to the company that did his professional work. Having refused Cousin Kevin's insistence that he should stay and keep her company, Laurel stood in the middle of the hallway.

The house seemed deathly quiet, but after the turmoil of the past few days, she welcomed the silence. Her friends had done such an excellent job of setting the house to rights that there was nothing for her to do. She changed into cotton pants and shirt and walked barefoot to the portico. Surprised at the peace that consumed her, Laurel sat in her favorite rocking chair and put her aching feet on a stool. She was weary to the bone, but she drew a deep, satisfying breath.

She must have gone to sleep, for she suddenly realized she wasn't alone, and she opened her eyes quickly. Micah stood at the foot of the steps.

"I thought I'd find you here. I won't be offended if you say you want to be alone, but I'm here if you want to talk."

"I'm not sure I want to talk, but come and sit with me." She held out her hand.

He clasped her hand tightly and took a chair close beside her. "Have you been crying?" he asked tenderly.

"Just a little, maybe. I don't know if you'll understand this, but actually, I'm glad the day is over. I've been dreading Debbie's leaving ever since she and Dereck became engaged. I suppose I've really been dreading it since the day she was born. I'm glad it's over."

"I was proud of you today," he said, and her eyelashes lowered from the love she saw in his eyes. "You must have been hurting, but you didn't show it. You seemed as happy as Debbie was, and if I may say it, you were as pretty as the bride. You looked radiant."

Laurel blushed. "I *was* happy. Debbie and I have entered a new relationship. I sent her off with the advice that Dereck should come first in her life now. I've come to terms with her leaving, and I have a new outlook for the future. I've lived my entire life for other people. After my parents were killed, I lived with my grandmother. Because she'd taken me in, I felt like I should be at her beck and call. After Jason was killed, I didn't want to stay at Oaklawn, but I felt guilty to take Debbie away from her grandparents, so I stayed on, thinking only of them and Debbie. Now I'm free to do what *I* want to do for a change, and I like it. Is that being selfish?"

"Not at all." Micah had thought that once Debbie was married, he could approach Laurel about his feelings for her. Now that he'd found the one and only woman to make him happy, he was eager to tell her so. But he decided that this wasn't the time to speak of his love and desire to marry her. Let Laurel enjoy her freedom a little while.

"You *should* have a life of your own," he agreed.

"That's what I think. I feel free for the first time in my life."

"Now that Debbie is married, would you consider contacting the police if the calls continue? Or your telephone company might be able to trace the calls."

"I don't know," Laurel said. "Perhaps I should. I'll think about it."

She yawned, and Micah stood. "I won't keep you any longer. But don't hesitate to call me if you need me. You know I'm a light sleeper."

Still holding her hand, he helped her stand.

"Knowing that will make me rest much easier. Thanks for everything, Micah. You've made a big difference this summer."

He tugged on her hand and she came closer. For a few days, Laurel would need a friend more than she'd needed to be presented with making a decision to marry or not to marry. Although he longed to do so much more, he simply held her close for a moment, so close that their heartbeats seemed as one. He kissed her hair and let her go.

The next few days, Laurel slowly adapted to her new role in life. She puttered with her flowers, sat often in the rose garden doing nothing. She walked to the river every day. She spent a lot of time reading the Bible, reveling in God's love for her. She memorized a verse from the first book of John. "God is love. Whoever lives in love lives in God, and God in him." And the more of God's love she received, the more Laurel was inclined to accept Micah's love. She knew he loved her because she had correctly interpreted the tenderness and glow that smoldered in his blue eyes.

Micah didn't approach her often, although she was conscious of his watchful eyes. He mowed the yard, and she was pleased with the smooth mat of grass that no longer showed the imprint of hundreds of footprints.

One day, when he returned from Knoxville, Micah brought her a copy of a magazine that carried the first article about his research in South America. He autographed the article with a flourish and handed it to her.

"Thanks!" Laurel said. "I'm flattered to know such a famous author. I'll enjoy reading it when I go to bed tonight. I like to read a while before I turn out the lights."

"I'm going to the apartment and read through the article to see if there are any printing errors. Nothing I can do about it now, but I want to be sure my words haven't been misconstrued."

"If you're free tonight, come for grilled steaks about six o'clock. I've been eating leftovers from the wedding dinner, and a steak will be a welcome change."

"Sounds good to me. I have some vegetables I need to use. I'll bring a salad."

"That will be great. I still have cake for dessert."

Micah stifled the jubilation he felt inside. He'd been wise to leave Laurel to her own thoughts for a few days. And he thanked God for giving Laurel the healing she needed. Making the salad took more time than he'd expected, so he hadn't finished reading the article before six o'clock. Micah carried the magazine with him and laid it on a chair while he took over cooking the steaks. Laurel put the plates on the table and ice in their glasses and chatted about the phone calls she'd received from Debbie and Dereck. She seemed rested and happy so Micah decided she'd had no more troubling communications from her harasser.

After they'd finished eating, he cleaned the grill while she carried dishes into the house.

"I didn't finish reading through my article," he said, "so I brought the magazine along. If you don't mind, I'll finish doing that here. This garden is such a pleasant place."

"I'd like for you to stay. The excitement of the wedding is wearing off now, and I'm getting lonely. My friends have been attentive—calling or dropping by for a few minutes. I know they're trying to help me. Most of the time I'm all right, but the quietness in the house is sometimes unbearable, especially at night. I'll bring my copy of the article and start reading it, too."

Laurel stretched out on the lounge, and Micah sat at the table with the magazine spread before him, a pencil in his hand. Before reading the text, Laurel turned the pages of the article looking at the pictures and reading the captions.

In one picture, a small monkey swung from a limb with both feet. The animal's mouth was open, a grin on its face, as if it enjoyed swinging. In another photo, Micah had caught a falcon descending with one outstretched wing toward its prey on the ground. She particularly liked the picture of a purple morning glory with a black insect fastened to its frail petals.

"You're an excellent photographer," she exclaimed. "I can't wait to see the wedding pictures. I'm sure they'll be wonderful."

"I hope so, but remember taking wedding pictures isn't my forte. I'd rather photograph landscapes and wildlife. I seldom feature pictures of people."

"But you have a picture of people on the last page of this article."

"That's the crew of scientists I worked with for over a year. I took that photo as we relaxed around the cook's tent after we'd worked all day. The editor thought a picture of the crew would be interesting."

"There are ten of you, including several natives."

He turned to the photo she'd mentioned. "That guy hunkered down in front of the group is the scientist in charge of the expedition. He's from Massachusetts, and he had an assistant from the United States, but the other naturalists were from South America. They hired natives to set up camp, haul baggage and cook for us."

"Micah!"

The alarm in her voice startled him.

"Who's the man standing apart from the group to the left of the picture? He's not a native!"

"That's Tex. If he had another name, I never heard it. He was an American, but he'd lived in Venezuela for years, and spoke Spanish as well as the natives. Most of the time I forgot he wasn't a native."

Laurel pulled on the collar of her blouse as if she was choking. Her skin had paled to a ghastly white, and she breathed unevenly. She looked ready to faint. With one fluid leap, Micah was kneeling beside her.

"My dear, what's wrong?"

She pointed at the picture, opening her mouth as if she was trying to speak and couldn't. Her eyes implored him.

"Is that your husband?" he asked with a sinking heart, remembering her husband had disappeared near the coast of South America.

She shook her head, and Micah experienced a sense of relief. She swallowed hard, but apparently she found talking difficult, for she shook her head and whispered, "It definitely isn't Jason, but it could be the friend that died with him. So if he's alive, Jason probably is, too." She dropped the magazine and buried her face in her hands.

Micah rubbed her tense shoulders. "Now don't jump to conclusions. It's been such a long time. How could you know what Jason's friend would look like now?"

"What else do you know about him?"

"Not much. He was a happy-go-lucky guy, pretty much of a loner. I thought he could have been more than a laborer if he'd wanted to be. He was with us for only a few months while we worked in the Venezuelan rain forest."

"That sounds like Ryan Bledsoe. He'd made a lot of money in the oil fields of Texas, and he quit working. He said he'd start working again when he ran out of money. Please, Micah, can you find out something about him?"

"I'll try, but the trail might be cold by now. We disbanded several months ago. Are you sure this is the man?"

"No, I'm not sure, but it could be. Somewhere I have a picture of Ryan Bledsoe and Jason taken on the day they were ready to leave on the sailing expedition. Jason sent it to his parents. I've got a stack of their photograph albums. I can look through them to find the picture."

"I'll help you, but first tell me what you can about the disappearance of your husband."

"Ryan Bledsoe owned a small sailboat. He and Jason took it down the coast of the United States and through the Gulf to South America. The wreckage of the boat washed ashore on an island in the Antilles, but there was no sign of Jason or his friend. The authorities traced the registration of the boat, and we eventually heard the news."

"Was the friend from this area?"

"No. His home was in Texas, but he had a cabin in the Blue Ridge Mountains. He and Jason did a lot of hiking on the Appalachian Trail. He was a happy-go-lucky guy without any close family. I resented my husband's friendship with him. Jason should have stayed at home and taken his responsibility as a father and husband, rather than jaunting around the world."

"And you've heard nothing else?"

She shook her head. "No. My father-in-law hired

Cousin Kevin to investigate, but he learned nothing. Apparently, both Jason and Ryan perished at sea."

Micah noticed that Laurel didn't exhibit any pleasure over the possibility that Jason Cooper might be alive, and he said as much.

"I don't mean to seem callous, but Jason and I weren't getting along very well when he died. We were happy until Debbie was born, but he seemed to resent her. He wasn't the one getting all the attention anymore. He wasn't a good father, but his parents praised him to Debbie, until she grew up thinking her father was superhuman. I didn't disillusion her. That may have been a mistake. If he is still living, it's hard to tell how he's turned out."

Because it was so important for his future happiness, Micah had to ask, "Then you're no longer in love with him?"

"No, and it shatters me to think I might have to continue as his wife. Debbie would be so happy to see her father that she'd never understand why I wouldn't be as overjoyed at his homecoming as she is. I might be in the position of either taking Jason back or losing Debbie."

"Then you wouldn't stay with him just to keep Oaklawn?"

She shook her head vehemently. "I love the house, and after all the work I've done on it, it would pain me to give it up, but I don't want the house if Jason goes with it."

Micah smothered a sigh. Another hitch in his plans

to ask Laurel to marry him. He knew this would have to be resolved before he could tell her he loved her.

"It's getting dark," Laurel said, "so we might as well go inside and look for that picture."

They went into the room where the piano was located, and Laurel knelt before a ceiling-high cupboard. The bottom shelves held the family albums.

"I'll start with the albums we've prepared since Debbie was born. Even though Jason didn't leave until two years later, I might have put that picture in one of those."

By eleven o'clock, they were still leafing through the albums, because Laurel stopped often to reminisce about some of the pictures. Micah was glad to see Debbie in the different stages of growth. Occasionally there was a picture of Laurel, and he was amazed to note how she'd stayed youthful through the years.

"Here it is," Micah said, pointing to a photo of two young men standing on the prow of a sailboat. At first glance, Micah saw a remarkable resemblance to the man he'd known as Tex. Most of the time Tex had worn a beard, but he would occasionally shave. Remembering those times, Micah thought that the man he'd known could be Ryan Bledsoe.

Tex had been a stocky, quiet, substantial individual. He had unruly dark hair, and as best as Micah could remember, he'd been secretive about his past. He'd done any job assigned to him without question, and he'd worked well. Micah hadn't had more than a half-dozen conversations with the man during the months he'd been with the expedition.

Laurel carefully compared the magazine picture to the one of Jason and Ryan Bledsoe. "It has to be the same man."

"I agree that the resemblance is remarkable."

"And when I was hoping for some peace of mind, this has to happen."

"Just because this man is alive doesn't mean that Jason is."

"I have to find out."

Micah knelt beside the cabinet and replaced the albums, except the one that Laurel held. "I know you do. I'll try to get in touch with the leader of that expedition and see what I can learn. It may take a few days. It's hard to tell where he might be now."

Chapter Twelve

Working through his agent, Micah learned that the scientist who headed the research group was presently working in a laboratory in Boston. He contacted the laboratory and was told that the scientist was away for a few days. A week passed before he was able to get in touch with the man. Both he and Laurel stayed busy, but felt they were simply marking time until they learned the identity of the man in the picture.

In the meantime, Debbie and Dereck settled into their Colorado apartment. The wedding pictures came and Micah arranged them into three albums—one for Laurel, one for Debbie and Dereck and one for Dereck's parents. Laurel mailed their albums by express mail, and she spent hours looking at the pictures, marveling at Micah's expertise in finding just the right pose and encouraging the right expression on the people he photographed. While one portion of her mind couldn't forget the possible existence of Ryan Bledsoe, she re-lived the happy days of Debbie's wedding.

Micah accepted a part-time position at the college to start after the first of the year. When the fall semester started, Micah sat in on several sessions. Laurel's ten-ants moved into their apartments for the winter. Leaves hinted of the beautiful foliage to come. And Laurel and Micah waited.

Finally, early one morning, Micah received the mes-sage they wanted when he opened his e-mail. He hus-tled over to the house and found Laurel, wearing a heavy sweater, sipping coffee on the back porch.

"I finally heard from the scientist, and he said that Kenneth Morrow is the name of the man we called Tex. He's an American, but he lives in a native village on a tributary of the Orinoco River in the interior of Venez-uela."

"Could he have changed his name?"

"Possibly."

With a long, exhausted sigh, Laurel said, "Even if he is Ryan Bledsoe, our chances of finding out are about as probable as finding a needle in a haystack. I guess we'll never know."

"We *are* going to find this man," Micah said, his arms encircling her. "This isn't the way I'd choose to propose to you, but I've been waiting several weeks for the right time to tell you I love you and want to marry you."

She hid her face on his shoulder.

"I believe you love me, too. Do you?"

She put her arms around his waist and nodded her head. His embrace tightened.

"I don't want another nod. I'd rather hear it from your lips. Would you like to become my wife?"

With a heart-wrenching sob, she said, "Yes."

He kissed her hair. "But you won't marry me until you're sure your husband isn't living. Am I right?"

Another sob. "Yes."

"After I've waited half my life to find the right woman for me, I won't sit here to wait and wonder. I'm going to South America to find Tex and see what he knows. I want you to go with me."

Laurel lifted a dismayed face to Micah. "I can't afford a trip like that."

"You won't have to. I'll pay. I could go alone and find out, but you'll have to know firsthand or you'll never be satisfied. I don't want a wife who lives in the past."

"I can't—" Laurel protested further, and Micah put his hand over her lips. She moved away from his hand. "I can't leave Oaklawn, wondering what might happen here."

"You *can!* Every excuse you come up with, I'll counteract it. Listen, Laurel, this is for our future happiness. You can ask one of your tenants, like Johnny, to stay in the house at night."

"But what will I tell Debbie? I don't want to get her hopes up that her father may still be alive."

"Write her a letter saying you and a friend are going

on a trip, and that you'll contact her in a few days. If things move as fast as I hope they will, we should be back in a week. She wouldn't have long to fret about it."

"I wouldn't consider doing that," Laurel said, her eyes snapping angrily. "It's obvious that you aren't a parent. If I can't tell her where I'm going and why, I won't go."

For a moment, Micah wondered if he was wise to want to marry someone whose temper was so unpredictable, but considering all the other things he loved about Laurel, he decided she was worth it. He'd just have to learn how to respond when she flew off the handle. Instinctively, he knew he shouldn't answer her in the same tone of voice she'd used.

He shrugged his shoulders. "All right, then," he said amiably. "I thought I was doing you a favor, but I guess not. I'll just forget about it. That will give me more time to work on my book."

He turned away and walked out the door and started toward his apartment.

He heard her steps behind him, and in a meek little voice she said, "Micah."

When he turned, her head was bowed and she wouldn't meet his eyes. "I'm sorry. I've been praying to control my temper, but it's hard for me. I appreciate your offer to help me, and I do want to go with you to South America, but I *must* tell Debbie. I try to treat other people the way I want to be treated. I'd want Debbie to tell me if she was going away."

He was amused at her meekness, but he said sternly, "If you want to be treated the same way you treat others, does that mean you want people to verbally assault you when you say something they don't like?"

She shook her head and turned toward the house.

Micah reached her in three long strides, took her by the shoulders and turned her into his arms.

"I don't intend to treat you that way. Tell Debbie about seeing the picture, and that we're going to see the man and find out what he knows about her father's death. Don't suggest that we expect to find her father."

"I won't." She looked up at him with penitent eyes. "Thanks for being so patient with me, Micah. Make arrangements that are convenient for you, and I'll go along. I'll write a letter to Debbie and mail it the day we leave."

"I'll get reservations as soon as possible, but let's make a few plans."

Micah released her and they went inside and sat at the kitchen table. "When can you leave?"

"It will take a few days. I'll have to let Pete and Brenda know we're going, too."

She could tell by the expression on his face that Micah wasn't pleased with her comment. Speaking as calmly as she could, she said, "I don't want to irritate you, Micah, but I can't leave without a lot of people knowing about it. This is a close-knit community—if I go away without telling them, my friends and neighbors would be worried. Especially since I've never gone away before."

"Can't you tell the Howes that you have to leave on a business trip without giving details? Otherwise, you'll have to make a lot of explanations, and I don't think it's wise with the vandalism you've had for everybody in the county to know you're away. And you shouldn't give any indication to anyone that your husband might be alive."

Lack of privacy was one of the things that disturbed him about settling down in this community. He'd never lived in an area where everybody knew every detail of what was going on in their neighbors' lives.

"You don't understand," she began.

"I'll admit that. I've lived pretty much to myself without giving an account to anyone about what I'm doing. Do what you have to."

"We're used to sharing our joys and sorrows."

"I don't understand such an attitude, but I'll accept it." He thought he'd have to if he married Laurel and settled down at Oaklawn. Would her love compensate for having his life on public display?

"I'll book our flights today, and then we'll get a passport for you. I'm assuming you don't have one."

"No. Doesn't that take a long time?"

"Generally speaking, it does, but it's possible to get one in twenty-four hours. However, I'll schedule our departure several days from now to be sure we have your passport. We'll make an application for the passport today at the county courthouse. You'll have to present the original or certified copy of your birth certificate and your driver's license. You also must have two photos, but we can get those at any photo shop."

Micah went to his apartment, and taking advantage of online services, he soon had their airline reservations. He next contacted a firm in Washington that could legally expedite the issuing of a passport. They assured Micah that they had the capacity to turn Laurel's documents around in time for them to leave before the weekend.

"We'll leave three days from now," he told her when he went back to the house. She sat on the back porch, doing nothing, and he sat beside her. "I left an open date for our return because I don't know how long it will take for us to find this man. We'll leave from the Knoxville airport at noon and arrive in Caracas, Venezuela, around eight o'clock in the evening. I've arranged for our rooms at the Hilton Caracas."

"I want to pay for my fare and hotel room."

He waved his hand, dismissing the idea. "This is all my idea, and we may be taking a wild-goose chase. I told you I'd pay for it." With a meaningful glance, he said, "I expect it to be worth the cost of the trip if we find out what we need to know."

"I trust you to do what's best."

"We'll get your passport application on its way today. You'll have to pay for the passport fees, so take your checkbook. Where's your birth certificate?"

"In my lockbox at the bank."

"We'll also go to the county health department.

You'll need tetanus and hepatitis shots. Maybe others, too, depending on your medical history."

Drawing a deep breath, Laurel said, "Looks like we'll have a busy day."

"We will, so let's get on the road."

Laurel's respect for Micah increased considerably as he skillfully guided her in every detail of their traveling plans. All summer, she'd considered him a quiet, laid-back man, but her admiration increased more and more as she witnessed his expertise as a world traveler.

They found a shop and had her photos made. She gasped when she saw the finished result, wondering if she really looked so ghastly, but she supposed the camera didn't lie. At the courthouse, Micah guided her in filling out the application. He'd prepared two letters of authorization to send to the passport company and had them ready for her to sign. Within a few hours, all of the necessary information was sealed in a FedEx envelope and on its way to Washington, D.C.

Before the day was over, Laurel began to understand what an exciting life she'd have if she married Micah. But after being a stay-at-home mom for years, how would she like traveling? Their lives had been so different, could they possibly have a happy marriage?

"Whee!" Laurel said when they got in his car to start home. "I feel like I've been in a tornado."

"And without any lunch, too." He looked at his

watch. "Only four o'clock, but I'm hungry. Let's stop and have a meal."

When they came to an Italian restaurant, Micah asked, "How about spaghetti or lasagna?"

"Suits me. Debbie didn't care much for Italian food, so I never prepare it at home. I often order spaghetti when I'm in a restaurant."

The cafe was small and homelike. They filled their salad plates at the bar, and while they ate, Laurel said, "I'm beginning to realize the enormity of what we're doing. I haven't even been on a plane or traveled in a foreign country. I don't have a clue about what I should pack and what kind of clothes I'll need."

"Haven't I seen you wearing a denim pantsuit?"

She nodded.

"That will be perfect for plane travel, and wear your most comfortable shoes. I've learned to travel light. And the destination always determines what kind of clothing to wear. If we have to go into the jungle to find this man, we'll be near the equator. It will be hot and muggy. You may want to take some shorts, but I think lightweight pants will be the best choice."

He reached out and touched her alabaster complexion. "You'll burn easily, so take plenty of sunscreen. Also bring body lotion, and insect repellant to protect your skin. You're fortunate your hair is naturally curly, or you'd be worried about damp, stringy hair."

Her eyes were pensive, and he took her hand. "Scared?"

"A little, but I'm excited, too, when I forget the reason we're going. I'm fortunate that the guide for my first travel adventure is an experienced traveler."

"We might have time for a little sight-seeing. Just depends on what we find out."

After they finished the meal and left the restaurant, Laurel said, "I don't have any luggage, so we should stop at the mall on our way home. It's been years since I've stayed away from home at night, and I don't have a suitcase. Debbie took all of hers."

Micah suggested a medium-priced large suitcase and a matching carry-on case, both on wheels for easy mobility. They soon found what she needed at the mall.

Although the day had been strenuous, Laurel wasn't able to sleep when she went to bed, knowing she was getting deeper and deeper in Micah's debt. But since he loved her, she understood why it was important for him to find the truth about Jason's death. It was comforting to have someone looking after her for a change. And although she missed Debbie, it was good to be carefree, able to go where she wanted to without considering others. Was that an un-Christian attitude? A selfish feeling? "God, forgive me if it's wrong," she prayed aloud. But God was understanding, and Laurel believed God agreed that, after being confined for years, she'd earned a little freedom.

Laurel phoned Pastor Jensen, telling him she was going away for a few days, and asked him to pray for her safety. He didn't ask for details and she gave none. She also called the Howes to let them know that she was leaving.

"I'm going with Micah on a business trip, but we won't be gone more than a week," she said to Brenda. When there was a sudden silence at the other end of the phone, Laurel said defensively, "Everything is on the up-and-up, so don't get any ideas."

Brenda laughed. "You don't have to justify your actions to me," she said. "You're over twenty-one, so I figure you can make your own decisions without my help. But Pete and I think you and Micah were made for each other. Don't let him slip away from you."

Brenda hung up softly before Laurel could think of a suitable retort.

Laurel felt obligated to tell Cousin Kevin something, and she was glad when he phoned the day before they were to leave to say that he would be out of town for a week. She thanked him for calling and felt justified in not mentioning her own trip. Hopefully, Micah and she would return before Kevin came home.

Chapter Thirteen

The passport arrived the day before they were to leave, and almost before she knew it, Laurel was standing in line at the Knoxville airport, nervous as a cat, but depending on Micah to tell her what to do. She showed her newly acquired passport for identification, checked her luggage and proceeded to the security checkpoint, hoping she hadn't packed the wrong things in her luggage. Micah had given her specific instructions about the items she couldn't carry on a plane. She'd followed his advice and she had no trouble. Once they'd both cleared security and were seated in the waiting room, Laurel sighed as she took a seat facing the runway.

Dropping his well-worn bag on the floor, Micah sat beside her and said softly, "I feel like somebody oughta be throwing rice at us."

Laurel darted an angry, suspicious glance toward him. He threw up his hands as if to ward off a blow.

"Just kiddin'," he said, and a quiver at the corner of his mouth alerted Laurel to the fact that he was needling her.

"I believe you say things just to make me mad," she accused.

"Not really, but I'll admit I do enjoy seeing your eyes blazing and that red hair crinkling as though you're going to explode."

She dropped her lashes, and two rosy spots brightened her cheeks. "I'm trying to control my temper."

Immediately contrite, he laid his hand on her shoulder. "I know you are, and I shouldn't tease you."

"Don't you ever get mad?" she asked.

"Yes, but I usually keep it inside and brood about it."

"That could cause an ulcer," she said worriedly. "At least, that's what I've heard."

"I don't get mad very often, so don't fret about it."

"I should have known you were teasing about the rice, but my conscience hurts a little. The Bible tells us to shun all appearance of evil, and I wouldn't want anyone to think we're doing anything wrong."

"I've been reading the Bible more this summer than I ever have before, and I ran across a verse recently. 'If our hearts do not condemn us, we have confidence before God and receive from Him anything we ask, because we obey His commands and do what pleases Him.' No matter what my natural inclination might be, you can be assured that I'll treat you as if you were one of my sisters from now until we get back to Oaklawn."

"I trust you, or I wouldn't have agreed to this trip, but I've been a little apprehensive about what could happen. I'm glad we brought this out in the open."

"I've arranged for adjoining rooms, but not connecting ones. If you should need me at night, you can call my room, and I can be with you right away."

"I'm a little worried about not being able to speak Spanish if we get separated."

"The only time you'll be out of my sight is when we're in our rooms at night. And in the larger hotels, most of the staff will speak English. You'll be all right."

Micah had asked for a window seat and an aisle seat, and he suggested that Laurel sit by the window. He quietly instructed her on fastening her seatbelt, and he stored their carry-on bags in the overhead compartment. Laurel was embarrassed that a woman of her age knew so little about matters that were everyday experiences for many people. But Micah didn't make her feel inadequate, and quietly assisted her, so their fellow travelers had no idea that this was her first plane trip.

The day was overcast, and Laurel was disappointed that as soon as the plane was airborne, her view of earth was obscured by cloud cover until they approached the Atlanta airport. Micah had explained about changing planes at the airport, and she had no trouble taking the escalator to the first floor, where they boarded a little train to the wing where the international flights departed. They had a two-hour wait for their plane to Caracas.

* * *

After they'd taken off from Atlanta, and were an hour into their flight, a meal was served, and although Laurel had often heard complaints about the poor quality of airline food, it was a novel experience. She enjoyed every bite of the garden salad, chicken and rice, mixed vegetables, roll and chocolate chip cookies. Her excitement amused Micah, but she didn't care. She'd waited over forty years to take a plane trip, and in spite of the outcome of their journey, she was having a good time.

Micah rented headphones, and they enjoyed a documentary on Venezuela, which prepared Laurel for the customs and scenery of the country.

"What are your plans once we get to Venezuela?" she asked when they removed the headphones.

"Kenneth Morrow spends most of his time in a remote village deep in Venezuela's rain forest, but he may have a residence in Caracas. Hopefully, we'll find Morrow in Caracas. If not, we can go into the jungle to find him. That may take several days."

Micah felt Laurel's body stiffen, and her eyes filled with concern. "How will we get into the jungle?"

"I have friends at one of the American oil companies operating in Venezuela. I can probably arrange for us to go in one of their helicopters to a landing strip at the edge of the rain forest. From there, the fastest way to the village is by boat."

"Oh, my!" Laurel said.

"You won't be afraid, will you?"

"I don't think so," she said hesitantly, "as long as you're with me. All of this is quite an adventure for a woman who's spent all of her life in Tennessee."

"It is quite an adventure, and it can be dangerous. But when you know what you're doing, you don't have to be afraid of the jungle. Even if I was alone, I wouldn't go to the interior without some natives for guides. We'll hire a couple of guides if we have to go that far."

A smile of affection and joy spread across Laurel's face, and Micah had to remind himself to treat her like a sister. "Thanks for giving me an opportunity to do this," she said.

With a quirk of his lips, which Laurel now recognized as his teasing look, he said, "Better not thank me until I have you back safe and sound at Oaklawn."

Laurel lifted her eyebrows impishly and favored him with a saucy grin. She was convinced that harm would come to her only over Micah's dead body.

The plane was late arriving in Caracas, and by the time they went through customs and took the shuttle to the hotel, it was eleven o'clock. The new experiences and the strange language frustrated Laurel. She was very tired, a little scared, and very uncomfortable if Micah was out of her sight. But he had no trouble communicating with the natives in their own language, and Laurel's fears abated.

In spite of her weariness, she was impressed by the spacious hotel. It was a far cry from the hotel she and

Jason had stayed in when they'd gone to Atlanta on their honeymoon years ago. Still, the strangeness of the city intimidated Laurel, and she was pleased to know that Micah would be next door.

Each room had a king-size bed, chairs, tables, a television enclosed in a large cabinet and a huge bathroom. Before he went to his room, Micah made sure she knew how to use the phone to call from room to room and explained the fire-escape system to her.

"It's been a few hours since we've eaten," Micah said, "and I ordered a light lunch of soup and fruit to be delivered to your room. I'll wait in my room until they bring the luggage, then I'll come here so we can eat together." As he started out the door, he cautioned, "Keep this security chain on the door, and don't let anyone in until you know who it is."

The luggage was delivered shortly before the food arrived, and to try using the phone, Laurel telephoned Micah's room to tell him the food was ready.

While they ate, Laurel exclaimed over the wall hangings, the massive furniture and the size of the room. "I'm surprised at such elegance," she said. "I thought there was a lot of poverty in Venezuela."

"There's a great deal of oil money in this country, and this hotel caters to affluent people. Compared to rates at home, this isn't an expensive hotel."

As soon as they ate their light lunch, Micah went to his room. "There isn't any reason to be afraid, but if you need me, call right away."

Laurel's body was weary, but she couldn't sleep at first. It had been years since she'd slept anyplace except Oaklawn, and the strange room was intimidating. She took a Bible from her luggage, and turning to one of her favorite Psalms, she read aloud,

"'Where can I go from Your Spirit? Where can I flee from Your presence? If I go to the heavens, You are there…. If I rise on the wings of the dawn, if I settle on the far side of the sea, even there Your hand will guide me, Your right hand will hold me fast.'"

The words reminded Laurel that no matter where she was, she wasn't separated from God's watchful eye. With that assurance, she went to sleep.

Since Venezuela was on the same time zone as Tennessee, Laurel woke at her usual time and for a moment she couldn't remember where she was. Without opening her eyes, she was conscious of the loud noise of traffic, and she knew she wasn't in the peaceful atmosphere of Oaklawn.

She thought about Micah's attentiveness, not only on this trip, but ever since he'd come to Oaklawn. She knew he would make a good husband, but she wondered if she loved him enough to become his wife. She didn't deceive herself that she was physically attracted to him. But considering her disastrous marriage to Jason, she knew she was hesitant to give herself to another man. She'd used her in-laws' disapproval as a reason for not dating, but she wondered if that was more of an excuse than a real reason. She was afraid to marry again. It was as simple as that.

She was startled by a knock on the door, and knew she'd fallen asleep again. She glanced quickly at the clock—seven o'clock.

Micah's voice was muffled by the door. "Are you awake, Laurel?"

She jumped out of bed and cracked the door. Micah was shaved and dressed for the day, and she said, "Oh, am I late? I'm sorry."

"There isn't much we can do for a few hours, but if you've had enough rest, go ahead and dress. Phone me when you're ready, and we'll go down to the restaurant for breakfast. By that time, I can make some telephone calls. Did you rest?"

"I couldn't go to sleep at first, but I must have slept well. I feel rested now."

Not wanting to delay him, Laurel hurried into the bathroom, but she couldn't resist soaking in the huge tub with her favorite lavender bath gel. Fortunately, it didn't take long for her to shampoo and dry her hair, and in less than an hour from the time she'd gotten out of bed, she tapped on Micah's door, ready for whatever adventure the day brought.

Micah let her in and made an involuntary appraisal of her appearance. She wore a pair of belted, flat-front khaki chinos, emphasizing that, in spite of having a married daughter and being in her forties, Laurel had the petite figure of a teenager. Her loose-fitting checked shirt was a vivid lime shade. She wore a pair of brown loafers. Her only jewelry was a pair of silver hoop earrings.

She squirmed a little under his scrutiny, and he said quickly, "You're looking great this morning."

"You said to dress for warm weather, but I brought a lightweight slicker like you suggested. Will I need it today?"

"No, but it will come in handy if we head into the jungle. Let's go eat breakfast."

After breakfast, they returned to their rooms about nine o'clock, and Laurel went into Micah's room while he made arrangements for their search. Kenneth Morrow's number was listed in the telephone book, and a woman answered when he dialed the number. Speaking in Spanish, he learned that the woman was the housekeeper, but that Mr. Morrow wasn't in residence. She was reluctant to give Micah any information, but finally said that he was in the jungle and wasn't expected home for two months.

Disappointed, he turned to Laurel and told her what he'd learned. "So we'll have to search for him."

"Since this man doesn't even have the same name as Jason's friend, this may be a wild-goose chase. But since we've come this far, let's try to find Kenneth Morrow."

"I'll make an appointment with a man I know at Allied Petroleum Offices and see if he can help us."

"Should I change into something more dressy?" Laurel asked.

"No. You look fine."

While he waited for a return call from the oil company, she went into her room and finished preparations for the day. When she returned to Micah's room, he had finished his conversation.

"We can see Mr. Sebastian in an hour. We'll take a taxi to his office."

The ride through the streets of Caracas in a taxi was an experience Laurel wouldn't soon forget. No one seemed to keep in a single lane of traffic, and the drivers shouted angrily at each other in Spanish. The drivers used their horns instead of brakes, and more than once she was thrown against Micah when the driver swerved to miss a pedestrian or another vehicle. Finally, he put his arm around her and held her close to his side.

"It's this way in all major cities of the world, although the cab drivers in this city are a bit more daring than most places."

"Let's walk back to the hotel."

He motioned to a few pedestrians trying to work their way across the street. "It's safer in a cab than trying to dodge vehicles on foot."

Nevertheless, Laurel was relieved to get out of the cab in front of a multistoried building. Here, too, Micah seemed to know his way around, and with his hand on her elbow, directed her inside to an elevator and pushed the button for the tenth floor.

When they stepped out of the elevator, Micah said, "We take the corridor to the left."

"I'm kinda scared, Micah. What if we find out things I'd be better off not knowing?"

"That's a risk you'll have to take. Now that there seems to be a chance to find out what happened to Jason, it's something you must do. Otherwise, you'll fret about it the rest of your life."

Micah opened the door to Mr. Sebastian's office and stepped back for Laurel to precede him inside. Laurel knew she was naive about the ways of the world, but surely this must be an outstanding reception area. The modern walnut furnishings, thick carpet, ornately framed oil paintings and a huge crystal chandelier were magnificent. One whole wall had windows extending from floor to ceiling, providing an exceptional view of the business district of Caracas with mountains in the background.

A receptionist rose from her desk with a quick fluid movement and spoke in Spanish.

"Mr. Sebastian said to show us in immediately upon our arrival," Micah repeated in English for Laurel's benefit.

Laurel had the sensation of sinking into thick turf as she walked across the room toward a connecting door. A handsome, middle-aged native rose from behind a huge desk and came forward to shake hands with Micah.

"Buenos días, Señor Davidson."

"Good morning," Micah said. "Señor Simon Sebastian, let me present my friend, Laurel Cooper. Mrs.

Cooper speaks no Spanish, so may we converse in English?"

"Of course," Mr. Sebastian said, with only a trace of accent.

He led them to a low table with several chairs grouped around it. The receptionist entered and placed a silver tray on the table. Another woman came with a tray of pastries.

The receptionist offered tea or coffee, and Laurel asked for coffee, as did Micah and Simon. The woman placed a pastry on each of the silver plates and left the room, closing the door behind her.

"Now what can I do for you, *señor?*"

"I'll need to relate a bit of background if you have time to listen."

Simon spread his arms wide in a Latin gesture, shrugging his shoulders. "I take the time for you, amigo."

"Mrs. Cooper's husband was killed in a boating accident off the coast of South America twenty years ago. He was sailing with a friend, Ryan Bledsoe. The wreckage of the sailboat washed ashore in the Antilles, but neither of the bodies was found. They were presumed dead. In my recently published article on the scientific expedition here on the continent, Mrs. Cooper saw a picture of a man she believes is the one who accompanied her husband on that boating trip."

Simon Sebastian looked at Laurel appraisingly before his eyes shifted back to Micah.

"After I talked with the scientist who headed our expedition, he told me the name of the man, and that he lives in Venezuela. Although he has a home in Caracas, the housekeeper told me this morning that he's in the jungle and won't be back for a few months. We want to see him. Mrs. Cooper is most anxious to see if he is her husband's friend, and if he knows what happened to her husband. His name is Kenneth Morrow, although that wasn't the name Mrs. Cooper knew him by. Can you help us find him?"

Mr. Sebastian's white teeth flashed in a large grin. "Yes, but I'm not sure I should. When he goes into the jungle, he doesn't want to be disturbed."

"You know him?" Micah said, startled by his statement.

"Why, yes, he's chairman of the board of Allied Petroleum."

Micah half rose from his chair. "It can't be the same man. The man I photographed was the camp flunky."

"Which probably *was* Señor Morrow. He says the only way he can keep sane in this rat race business world is to lose himself for a few months in the jungle, mostly in the village of Twanke."

Concern mirrored on his face, Micah turned to Laurel. "If he's off with another expedition like ours, we won't be able to follow him, Laurel. For weeks at a time, we didn't have contact with the outside world."

Micah looked disappointed, and Laurel knew she was. "We can't stay here for weeks," she said.

"I know, but he may be in the village." Micah turned to the other man. "Simon, I'm going to make a request, and if it violates company policy, don't hesitate to say so. If you're sending a supply plane to your Orinoco River drilling site soon, would there be room for Laurel and me to catch a ride that far? From there, we can probably hire some guides to take us by boat into the jungle. If we can't find Morrow, we'll return home, knowing that we've at least tried."

With a knowing glance from Micah to Laurel, Simon smiled broadly, saying, "And finding out what Morrow knows is of utmost importance to you, no?"

"Of utmost importance," Micah replied. "I want Laurel to marry me, but she won't commit until she knows what really happened to her husband."

"We have a helicopter leaving for the camp early tomorrow morning. And not only will I arrange passage for you, but when you get to the camp, I'll order two of our native workers to take you and Mrs. Cooper in a motor launch to the village."

"Will this make trouble for you?"

"Señor Morrow is a reasonable man. If he's the one you're looking for, I believe he would want to help you."

Simon moved to his desk and made two telephone calls, speaking in Spanish, so Laurel didn't understand what he said. When he terminated the last conversation, he said, "You're to be at the company's landing field west of the city by seven o'clock tomorrow morning. You know where it is, no?"

Micah nodded.

"I'll send written orders for your transportation to Twanke. Take what you need for an overnight stay. I don't know how long it will take to reach the village, and even if you see Mr. Morrow right away, you won't get back to our camp in time to return to Caracas tomorrow night."

"Do you have helicopters back and forth to the camp every day?"

"Not always, but the chopper that takes you will remain until you're ready to return."

Micah shook hands with Simon before they left, and Simon bowed to Laurel. She extended her hand, and he surprised her by lifting her hand to his lips and brushing it lightly with his lips. "I'll expect an invitation to the wedding," he said, smiling broadly.

Chapter Fourteen

Laurel wished they could have continued their journey immediately when it seemed there was a possibility of learning what really happened to Jason, but the day passed more quickly than she anticipated.

They took a cab to tree-shaded Plaza Bolivar, and Micah hired a guide to walk with them through the historic colonial district. Laurel learned a lot of Venezuelan history as they visited Simon Bolivar's birthplace, the Capitol and the presidential palace. They appreciated the early efforts of Spanish missionaries after they visited the Basílica de Santa Teresa, with one facade dedicated to Saint Ann and the other to Saint Teresa. After lunch in a sunlit sidewalk café in the Sabana Grande district, Micah took her shopping.

Always mindful of her limited budget, Laurel did more looking than buying.

"I want to buy something for Debbie and the

Howes," she said. "What would be a typical Venezuelan gift?"

"I'm not an authority on souvenirs," Micah said, "but we'll look around."

He took her into a shop offering gifts of all kinds— some imported items, but most of them made within the country. She passed by the jewelry, knowing she couldn't afford that, and looked instead at the hardwood carvings, pottery and baskets. She liked them, but they would be too difficult to take home on the plane. She instead chose two woolen tapestries depicting Venezuelan native culture, which she could easily pack in her luggage.

While she shopped and finally made her purchases, Micah spent his time in the jewelry area. When she joined him, he was carefully inspecting a diamond ring in a white gold setting. The two-carat stone glistened like sun on fresh-fallen snow as Micah turned it in the light.

"The diamond was mined in this country. What do you think of it?"

Suppressing her natural instinct to exclaim over its beauty, she said quietly, "It's very nice."

His eyebrows arched provocatively. "Nice! Is that all you can say about it?"

"Yes."

"Try it on," he said, and she shook her head.

"You're embarrassing me. I haven't made any definite promises."

"Not with your lips, perhaps, but your eyes have made many promises. And there's no reason to be embarrassed. Most of these people don't know what we're saying."

He took her left hand and slipped the ring on her third finger. "How does that feel?"

"Please don't, Micah."

"Just consider it a souvenir of our first trip together," he said. "You're not obligated any further than that."

He handed the ring to the clerk, who'd been watching them closely, and said something in Spanish. The woman lifted Laurel's hand and took the measure of her finger and made an observation. He took out his credit card and paid for the ring. Laurel turned her back, glad for once that she couldn't understand Spanish. She didn't want to know what it cost.

"It will be at least an hour before the ring is ready," he said. "Anything else you want to buy?"

She shook her head. Micah took her package, saying, "Let's find a cab and go to Mount Avila National Park. The mountain is over seven thousand feet above Caracas, and we can ride in a cable car to get a good view of the city."

As they drove to the summit of the mountain, Micah knew that Laurel had exceeded his hopes as a good traveler. She hadn't hesitated to do anything he'd suggested. He thought she might balk at riding in a chopper, but she hadn't questioned it. She'd tried native foods and liked them, and even now, she perched on the edge of the seat and peered out the windows, unwilling to miss anything.

The cable-car ride was a short one, but it was wonderful to have a bird's-eye view of Caracas. Laurel identified several of the places they'd visited earlier in the day.

The cab took them back to the jewelry store, and after she tried on the ring, Micah said, "I'll have the clerk wrap the box, since you'll have to wait a while to wear it. We'll leave all of our jewelry, and most of our money, in the hotel's safe tonight. You can wear your watch, but give me everything else of value, and I'll put them in a leather container I have. They'll be safer in the big safe in the office, rather than the small ones in our rooms."

Laurel was glad he didn't insist that she start wearing the ring immediately. Regardless of what they learned at the village, she couldn't envision herself returning to Oaklawn with that huge diamond on her finger. For the first time, she wondered about Micah's finances. She wouldn't have thought that a freelance photographer journalist would make a whole lot of money, but Micah didn't seem concerned about the cost of anything.

When they returned to their hotel rooms, Laurel realized that the day she'd been dreading had passed quickly. She took Micah's hand. "You're so good to me. I thought this would be a long day, but we've done so many interesting things I've seldom thought about what I might find out tomorrow. Thanks."

"I've enjoyed the day as much as you have, so consider the experience as my desire to please you."

"You have," she said, as they continued to hold hands.

"Now tell me what I should wear tomorrow."

He walked into the room with her.

"It will be hot and damp in the jungle, but you should wear long pants and a long-sleeved shirt or jacket. Pack an extra change of clothes and shoes in your small suitcase. We need to travel light. Take insect repellant, sunscreen and lotion, but forget about makeup." He surveyed her soft complexion with a smile. "You don't need it anyway. I'm not releasing the rooms, so leave anything you don't want to take in your room."

Laurel winced inwardly. She had seen the room rates on the doors. She was getting deeper and deeper in Micah's debt.

"I'll order a light breakfast delivered to our rooms at five. We have to be ready to leave the hotel at six. Since Simon's doing us a favor, I don't want to be late."

Laurel moved close to Micah, and with a shy smile, put her hands on his shoulders and stood on tiptoes to kiss his cheek. "I've seen so little of the world that today has been an educational experience, but it's been a fun day, too."

Micah had been determined to keep their relationship light because he didn't want Laurel to be concerned, but since she'd opened the door, his arms automatically went out and he pulled her into a strong embrace. She lifted her lips with a willingness that brought a yearning to Micah's heart. He kissed the long lashes that shielded her eyes from his questioning gaze, then he trailed a row of kisses down her cheek. He stopped short of her lips, put her gently away from him and turned to the door.

"Is that the way you kiss your sisters?" she teased.

"No, but I might if they tempted me like you did."

"I'll be good from now on," she said.

"Don't bother. I like you the way you are."

Because of the early hour and the lack of traffic, the cab ride to the airport wasn't as harrying as the one the previous day. Laurel both anticipated and dreaded the journey ahead of her. For one thing, she'd noticed a bulge in Micah's shirt, and he admitted that he was wearing a holstered gun. When she'd asked if he expected danger, he'd assured her that it was just a precaution against wild animals. She was convinced he wouldn't take her into a place that was extremely dangerous, so she decided to take each new experience as it came. She was eager to ride in the helicopter and to see the rain forest, but she dreaded the outcome of the meeting with Kenneth Morrow.

One minute, she hoped he was Jason's friend and could shed some light on the disappearance of her husband. Then immediately, she wondered if she should have left well enough alone.

When they arrived at the airport, little more than a

landing strip with a few buildings and hangars, an American pilot, Sam, greeted them, took their luggage and handed it to a native worker. The helicopter was nearby, the chopper blades circling slowly, the engine sounding loud in the quiet of the morning. Red lights blinked on the top of the aircraft.

Laurel thought her face must mirror her trepidation because the pilot's mouth twitched in a smothered smile, when he said, "Your first copter ride, ma'am?"

She nodded and darted a quick look at Micah, who also looked amused. Taking a deep breath, she managed a smile. "But I'm looking forward to it."

Making no effort to conceal their amusement, Micah and the pilot laughed loudly. Refusing to take offense, Laurel laughed, too. "I *am* looking forward to it," she insisted.

"Let's go, then," Sam said, and Micah and Laurel followed him. The wind generated by the big blades nearly swept Laurel off her feet, and she reached for Micah's hand. He steadied her and assisted her up the steps into the helicopter. The co-pilot smiled at her when she sank breathlessly into a seat behind him. She and Micah were the only passengers, but the large aircraft was filled with boxes and cartons of provisions.

The noise of the engine increased as the copter lifted off the ground. In spite of the headsets they wore, Laurel soon realized that this flight wasn't going to be as noiseless and smooth as their trip on the jet from Atlanta to Caracas. The copter flew close to the ground, and Laurel could see the terrain below them.

Micah leaned close to her and explained what they saw. They flew over tracts of virgin forests containing prime hardwood timber. Some forested areas had been denuded by slash-and-burn farmers from which nutrients were exhausted after only a few crops. Many acres had been cleared for cattle ranches, and Laurel saw white cattle grazing amid the skeletons of the old forest.

After more than an hour's flight, Sam looked around at them and pointed downward, indicating they'd reached their destination. The clearing, full of drilling equipment and several buildings, was ringed by the forest. The drone of the chopper's engine had caused Laurel's ears to ring, and she was slightly dizzy when she walked down the steps. She gladly took hold of Sam's hand as he reached out to steady her.

Sam directed them to the lounge of the administration building, and the business manager served them coffee and sent a co-worker to the kitchen in a separate building to fetch some sandwiches. Laurel looked around timidly for a restroom, but it must have been an all-male operation, because she didn't see a separate restroom for ladies.

Laurel wondered if the manager had read her thoughts, because he said, "If you need to refresh yourselves, there's a washroom at the end of this hall. Your boat is ready whenever you want to leave. Mr. Sebastian sent word to provide you with a boat, two guides, a hamper of food and sufficient water for several days. Is there anything else we can do for you?"

Micah assured the man that Mr. Sebastian had been very thorough in providing for their needs. Laurel was in a hurry to get on her way, but Micah knew the customs of the country, and he spent an hour eating and talking with the business manager.

The motor launch provided plenty of room for the four of them and their provisions. Micah put on a life jacket and helped Laurel into hers. He handed her a tube of insect repellent. "Put on a lot of it," he said as he lavishly applied the cream to all his exposed body parts. They sat facing each other in the middle of the boat. One guide sat at the stern of the boat to operate it, while the other knelt in the front to spot any dangerous obstructions in the water.

Water churned behind them as the engine roared and the guide directed the boat into the water. Laurel held tightly to the side of the boat, but her eyes glowed with enjoyment.

The stream was narrow, and after a few miles, the jungle closed around them. The dense foliage made a canopy over their heads, shutting out the sunlight. Big tree ferns, some ten feet tall, stretched their long delicate fronds toward the sky. Many trees had thick roots spreading out from the base of the trunk. Large vines, climbing up the trees toward sunlight, helped to knit the canopy together. The trunks of some trees were so twisted that they seemed to be in agony, but along these branches grew ferns, orchids, mosses and dozens of other plant species. Some trees towered to a height of over two hundred feet, and the green foliage of their branches and treetops spread out like a huge umbrella to shade the forest floor. They traveled in semidarkness part of the time.

When Laurel's eyes adapted to the strange light through the gaps in the foliage, she saw brightly plumed birds flying from tree to tree. Although at first the forest seemed quiet, Laurel's ears soon became attuned to the drone of insects, the songs of smaller birds, and the incessant prattle of parrots. Long-tailed monkeys wrapped around tree trunks and watched the boat's progress.

A brightly spotted jaguar lay on a branch over the river and scooped fish out of the water with its sharp claws. A lizard skimmed across the surface of the stream, rearing up on its hind legs and using its tail for balance. Turtles rested on semisubmerged tree trunks, and snakes slithered through the water, evading the boat.

Mile after mile, they saw nothing except the jungle, and Laurel's eyes grew weary with all of the new sights. Micah watched her closely for signs of fear, and he saw none. He silently thanked God for her reaction to this new life. Adventure was in his blood, and he couldn't be content to settle permanently within the narrow confines of Oaklawn. Laurel was obviously a suitable companion to share his adventurous life, and he prayed that what they learned today would give him the pleasure of introducing her to the wonders of the world he'd enjoyed.

Micah's last doubt that Laurel would be a mate who'd share his adventures vanished. Pensively, he wished he'd found her years ago, and they could have had a lifetime together.

They traveled two hours before they came to the village of Twanke, located directly on the river. Laurel was amazed to see another motorboat similar to theirs. Micah thought belatedly that he should have prepared her for the village life they'd soon encounter.

The village consisted of huts built on strong stilts to protect them from the damp forest floor. Some of the buildings were enclosed with a framework of thin branches and a roof of thatched leaves. The larger buildings were communal huts where the preparation and consumption of food were held in common. Micah explained that the smaller, enclosed huts were dwellings, and that the village holdings probably extended several miles into the forest. Chickens and dogs wandered around the area.

Laurel was unprepared for the amount of nudity she saw. Both men and women were bare-chested. The women wore thigh-length skirts, and the men brief loincloths.

Micah couldn't speak the language, but when one of the guides inquired for Kenneth Morrow, they learned that he was out hunting, but was expected back today. Micah and Laurel returned to the launch and ate some of the food provided for them by the cook at the petroleum camp.

Soon a crowd of naked children sat on the bank watching them. The children looked well-fed, but their scrutiny disturbed Laurel. "Do you suppose they're hungry? Maybe we should share our food."

"Their diet agrees with them more than our food would. I won't risk giving the children something that might make them sick."

"But what could they eat? I don't see any gardens."

"They cultivate corn and beans, but they also live off the forest food—iguana eggs, smoked iguana meat, wild nuts, berries and—" he added with a fiendish grin "—juicy grubs and large ants eaten alive."

Laurel's stomach knotted. "Micah! Have you ever eaten those things?"

"Will it be held against me if I have?"

She shook her head.

"Our cooks on the expedition prepared a lot of the jungle foods, and they're tasty, but I did pass on the grubs and live ants."

After they'd finished eating, Micah left the company employees to guard the boat so he and Laurel could walk around. They came to a small pond that was covered with a type of water lettuce shaded by the skeleton of a dead tree. A large group of egrets had settled on its big branches, and the noise was horrendous. They walked almost in semidarkness because the thick foliage obscured the rays of the sun, causing it to appear that night was approaching. Laurel sensed that Micah was uneasy because he kept glancing at his watch.

When they came to a thick wall of jungle growth, they turned and walked slowly back toward the river. Micah wanted to be on hand when Morrow came. If he didn't show up soon, they'd have to spend the night in the village. For Laurel's convenience, he would have preferred to return to the petroleum camp before nightfall.

They'd rested on the launch for about an hour, when some of the children started running into the forest, shouting. One of their guides said in broken English, "Señor Morrow and warriors return."

Micah and Laurel left the boat and walked to the center of the village.

Two warriors led the procession carrying a small deer slung between two poles, and behind them two other men also carried a deer. Several men followed them, and the village inhabitants soon intermingled with the returning hunters. A brawny white man, wearing only a loincloth, stopped in his tracks when he saw Micah and Laurel. His face was covered with a thick growth of black whiskers. More slowly, he approached them.

"Do you recognize him?" Micah said quietly to Laurel.

"I don't know. It's been twenty years. Ryan Bledsoe didn't have facial hair when I knew him."

"You took me by surprise, Mr. Davidson," Morrow said in Spanish. "I didn't recognize you at first."

Obviously, Morrow was the man he'd known on the expedition, but whether he was Jason's friend was yet to be determined. Answering in English so Laurel would understand, Micah said, "Then you *are* the man who was on our expedition, who called himself Tex."

Morrow threw down the lance he was carrying, and a woman rushed to take the pack from his shoulder. He glanced at the company barge and lifted his hand toward the two guides.

"I've had many names," he said in English, and his eyes shifted to Laurel. "Why have you come?"

"I apologize for forcing our company on you," Micah said, "and please don't hold it against your staff for bringing us here. It's a matter of great importance, and after we'd come to South America to see you, I didn't want to go home without contacting you. We understood that you weren't expected back in Caracas for a few months, so I contacted Simon Sebastian for help. If you can tell us what we need to find out, or if you're not the man we're looking for, we'll leave right away."

Morrow looked at Laurel appraisingly.

"This is my friend, Laurel Cooper. She thinks you can give her some information about her husband."

Morrow's astonishment was apparent, but soon recognition dawned and a thoughtful smile curved his mouth. "It's been a few years, Mrs. Cooper, and you've weathered those years better than I have." He gazed at the darkening sky. "But you can't leave tonight."

Worried, Micah said, "I know that now. We've been waiting several hours for you to return."

"The natives will be feasting tonight and it will be an all-night affair, but I'll guarantee your safety. It may be a little noisy, Mrs. Cooper, but you'll be safe enough. If you'll give me a short time to bathe and shave, I'll be at your service the rest of the evening."

Laurel clutched Micah's hand as they watched Morrow enter a large hut. One of the native women followed him. "I'm afraid, Micah."

"No need to be. Morrow will keep the natives away from us."

"Oh, as long as I'm with you, I'm not afraid of the people. I fear what he'll tell us. I've lived with mystery for twenty years, and now that I'm going to learn about Jason, I'm terrified."

"I understand. But whatever we learn, we'll deal with it together." His eyes brimmed with tenderness and compassion, and when he squeezed her hand, her fears lessened.

Laurel would never forget that evening.

While the natives butchered the deer and hung the carcasses on a tripod over a smoldering fire, she and Micah sat on the ground near the river with Kenneth Morrow, now smoothly shaved and dressed in Western garments. She'd seen Ryan Bledsoe only a few times when he came to Oaklawn. Without the picture, she wouldn't have been sure who he was, but he was definitely the man who'd stood beside Jason in the sailboat.

Micah explained about the article he'd written, saying that Laurel had seen his picture and believed he was the person who'd supposedly died with Jason Cooper in the boating accident. If *he* was alive, perhaps her husband might be, too. They'd come to South America to learn what they could.

"I have a daughter," Laurel explained, "who would like to know what happened to her father. Is Jason alive and living here in South America, too?"

Morrow eyes registered amazement. "I survived the accident, but Jason didn't. Weren't you notified that his body was recovered?"

Micah's blue eyes met her green ones in a compelling, magnetic glance.

Laurel shook her head. "We were notified that the wreckage of your boat washed ashore in the Antilles. One of Jason's cousins tried to find out more information, but we couldn't learn anything."

"I'm very sorry, Mrs. Cooper, that you've had to live in doubt all of these years. Jason and I were able to get into a lifeboat when the ship wrecked, and we washed ashore in a small village near San Juan, east of Caracas. Jason was dead when we were rescued, and I had received a severe head injury."

He pulled back his heavy hair and revealed a jagged scar across his forehead. "I lost my memory, and it was two years before most of my past came back to me. By that time, I'd taken the name of Kenneth Morrow. The people who'd rescued me told me where Jason was buried. I would have contacted you, but had no idea you didn't know what had happened."

"Do you know where his grave is?"

"Yes. I had a marker placed a few years ago. I'll go back to Caracas with you and show you where the grave is."

"And you've lived in South America since then? Didn't you want to return home?" Laurel asked.

"Not to live. I have made a few business trips to the States. I had nothing to return for except a lot of money. I was in my early twenties when I inherited some money from my grandfather. I invested that money in the Texas oil fields and made a fortune. People only wanted to be around me because of my money. I invested my money, left Texas and traveled to get away from riches. Jason and I got along fine, because he didn't ask anything about my finances. He was the only real friend I had."

Bitterly, Laurel thought that Jason should have been with his family instead of traveling around the country, but she said nothing, and Kenneth Morrow continued.

"I like Latin American ways, and I liked the new name I'd taken when I couldn't remember my own. I went to work in the oil fields, and gradually my memory returned. In the States, I'm still Ryan Bledsoe. I invested some of my money in this country, and would you believe I struck it rich again? Money means nothing to me, yet everything I touch turns a profit. I prefer to work with my hands rather than to make business decisions. I get so sick of affluence that two or three times a year, I leave it all behind and live in the jungle where money can't buy anything."

"I don't want to disturb your time off," Laurel said. "If you can tell us where the grave is, we can probably find it."

"I want to go with you, Mrs. Cooper. I'm sorry I can't offer you a comfortable place to sleep tonight. You'll be perfectly safe if you sleep in my hut."

Laurel didn't want to sleep out of Micah's sight, but she looked to him for the decision.

Discerning her wishes, Micah said, "Your employees provided two sleeping bags for us. Laurel can sleep on the launch, and I'll sleep on the bank beside the boat."

"Whatever makes you comfortable," Kenneth Morrow said. "We'll leave at daybreak."

"Good night, and thank you," Laurel said, giving him her hand.

"Anything I can do to help you. I've always felt guilty that I persuaded Jason to leave his wife and child to accompany me on that trip. I've wondered occasionally what had happened to you."

"I'm still living at Oaklawn. Jason's parents left the property to me. My daughter was married there two weeks ago."

"I'm glad life turned out well for you," he said, then abruptly turned on his heel and went toward the group huddled around the fire, waiting for the meat to cook.

Micah and Laurel gazed after him. "An odd way for a millionaire to live," Micah said.

"I never knew why he and Jason got along so well, but I understand it better now. Jason was a loner, too. Thanks for bringing me on this trip, Micah. Kenneth Morrow has lifted a burden off my back that's been lying there for years."

Micah moved a few items, spread Laurel's sleeping bag on the floor of the launch, and tucked her into it. He kissed her good-night, and she clung to him.

"Are you scared?" The dim light from the fires revealed the concern in his eyes.

Laurel remembered the water snakes and the many large insects she'd observed during the boat trip. In spite of the trouble she'd had at home, she longed for her bed at Oaklawn. But not wanting to add to Micah's concern, she smiled brightly.

"Not as long as you're close by."

"I'll spread my bed beside the boat. I'm easy to rouse. You'll be all right."

The natives feasted throughout the night, and when the sound of drums rolled through the clearing and the reveling increased, Micah knew they were drinking their fermented brew. He rolled up his sleeping bag and stepped quietly into the launch. Laurel sat up quickly.

"It's Micah," he said.

"What's going on?" she said. "All that shouting woke me."

"They're drinking some homebrew liquor. I'm going

to sit in the launch. I can't sleep anyway. Don't be afraid."

"He said I'd be all right."

"And I'm sure you will," Micah said. He placed his sleeping bag in the bottom of the boat and sat on it, stretching his legs beside Laurel. If anyone tried to come into the boat, they'd stumble over his legs, and that would rouse him if he should fall asleep. He probably shouldn't have brought Laurel into the jungle, but her next words put that thought to rest.

Placing her hand on his ankle, she said, "Micah, if I had a choice of any place I'd rather be tonight, you know where it would be?"

"Where?"

"Right here with you," she said softly. "The gentle movement of the boat as it swayed with the river's flow rocked me to sleep. I did my mourning for Jason years ago, so I'm happy now that we know what really happened to him. It's dark here in the jungle, but it's daybreak for you and me."

Chapter Fifteen

Laurel had never had any desire for riches. But the next twelve hours, when Kenneth Morrow maneuvered them quickly and efficiently from the jungle to Caracas, proved that an abundance of money could be advantageous.

When Kenneth came to the dock soon after daylight, Laurel and Micah were ready to go. They'd walked back and forth along the riverbank for about fifteen minutes to ease their cramped muscles.

Kenneth was dressed in a pair of trousers and a shirt, and he was accompanied by three natives. One of them jumped into the other motor launch and started the engine, but when they started downriver, Kenneth handled the boat.

The return trip to the oil company's site seemed shorter than the trip upriver. Sam greeted them, and Kenneth told him to prepare the helicopter for immediate departure. At the landing field in Caracas, a limousine met them and whisked them to their hotels. Kenneth Morrow told them he'd come for them again in two hours, and Laurel was glad for that time to take a bath and put on clean clothing.

As they waited in the hotel lobby for his return, Micah bought a bouquet of fresh flowers and gave them to Laurel.

"For Debbie," he said, and Laurel nodded her thanks.

Three hours later, she stood in the cemetery in a village churchyard near the town of San Juan. When they'd arrived at the cemetery, Micah had stayed near the gate while the other man took Laurel to the grave site. Under the circumstances, he thought Laurel would prefer to be alone to say this last goodbye to her husband.

Laurel clutched the flowers, and tears welled in her eyes as she read the tombstone inscription, Jason Cooper. And beneath his name, a quotation by Aristotle. "Without friends no one would choose to live, though he had all other goods."

"I didn't remember his birth date," Kenneth Morrow apologized. "There are some things about the past I've never recalled."

Laurel nodded. "You've done well. Without you, I'd never have found his grave."

Twenty years! All those years when she'd had to be both mother and father to Debbie, Jason had been lying in this lonely grave, so far from home. Although Jason had killed all the love she'd ever had for him, pity welled up in her heart for his parents who'd died mourning their only son, and for Debbie who'd missed so much by not having a father.

Swallowing hard and biting back her tears, Laurel knelt and laid the flowers beside the marker. But overcome by the finality of this moment, and wishing that Debbie could be with her, she yielded to compulsive sobs and tears that slowly found their way down her cheeks.

Unable to stay aloof from her sorrow any longer, within a few seconds Micah was on his knees beside her, his right arm wrapped around her midriff. She turned and buried her face against his shoulder, comforted by Micah's caring hands smoothing her hair. She pulled away, and Micah helped her stand. He wiped her tears with his handkerchief as Laurel looked at the surroundings.

The cemetery was well cared for, and Laurel was thankful that Kenneth Morrow had preserved Jason's memory. Perhaps someday Debbie could visit her father's grave. She supposed she could have the remains exhumed and taken to the United States for reburial, but that would be more expensive than she could afford. And she didn't dare mention it, or Micah might think she was hinting.

"You're convinced that these are Jason's remains?" Laurel asked Kenneth Morrow.

"Only to the extent that the people who rescued me said that the body of the man buried here was on the lifeboat with me. It couldn't have been anyone else."

Micah had picked up his camera at the hotel and

brought it with them. "Do you want a picture of the grave?" he asked.

"Yes, for Debbie. And a picture of the church in the background. Thanks again for buying the flowers."

"Mrs. Cooper," Kenneth Morrow said. "If you'll permit me to do this, I'll arrange to have Jason's remains exhumed and sent to the United States."

"Oh, it's kind of you to offer, but I won't impose on you. This is a quiet place to be buried. It's all right."

"Really, I insist. I've told you that I have more money than I know what to do with. I have citizenship in Venezuela as well as in the United States. It won't be as difficult for me to handle this matter as it would be for you. And although I don't have any doubt of it, I'll order DNA testing, so you'll know for sure that this is Jason's body."

"But, it's—"

"I want to do this. In the year we traveled together, Jason and I became good friends. I want to do it for him, as well as for you and your daughter, but I have to have your permission."

"Very well. I accept your offer. Jason's parents mourned to the end of their days that their son wasn't buried in the family cemetery. Debbie will be pleased to have her father buried at Oaklawn."

"When we return to Caracas, I'll put my lawyers to work on this. When do you plan to leave?" he asked Micah.

"We won't leave until you have these arrangements made."

"I can have any necessary papers ready for you to sign tomorrow."

"Then we'll leave the following day."

When the limousine stopped in front of their hotel, both Laurel and Micah expressed their thanks to Kenneth Morrow for the help he'd given them.

Offering him her hand, Laurel said, "You've lifted a burden from my heart that's been there for years. It's hard to find closure for a death without a body."

"I may not see you before you leave, but I'll be in touch by telephone. My attorney will bring the necessary papers to your hotel."

Micah and Laurel stood on the sidewalk and watched the limousine drive away.

"I feel sorry for him," Laurel said as they walked into the hotel.

"It's pretty hard to feel sorry for a man who's a multimillionaire, but I agree with you. Maybe he finds contentment at Twanke village, but I doubt it."

Stepping into the elevator that would take them to their rooms, Laurel asked timidly, "Do you think he's married to one of those women?"

"I'm sure he lives with one of them. I saw two children with near white features, and they looked like Morrow."

Micah opened the door into her room, and Laurel took a deep, steadying breath as she slumped in one of the upholstered chairs. "Since we left home, my emotions have been skyrocketing. Now I feel like I'm on a downhill slope."

"Don't collapse yet," Micah said with a laugh, taking her hand and lifting her upward. Holding her at arm's length, he said, "Before we left Oaklawn, you admitted you loved me and wanted to marry me, but not as long as you thought your husband was alive." She lowered her heavy lashes, but Micah lifted her chin so that her eyes met his. "Are you satisfied now that you've been a widow for twenty years?"

"Yes," she said softly. Her lids came down swiftly over her eyes once more.

"Look at me," Micah said, and when she looked up, he continued, "Will you marry me?"

"Yes."

Her lashes fluttered down again before his yearning gaze, but when he gathered her close, she lifted her mouth with eagerness, and he kissed her again and again. Laurel's heart pulsed rapidly, and when his lips released her, she stared up at him in astonishment. A half smile hovered about his lips, and his eyes glowed with his love for her. She had never believed that love could be so tender and sweet, but at the same time, so thrilling and all-consuming.

"Oh, yes, Micah, I *do* want to marry you."

He released her reluctantly. "Then we'll make plans as soon as we return to Oaklawn."

As the plane lifted from the runway of the Caracas airport, the events of the past few days seemed almost like a dream to Laurel. It was less than a week since they'd left Oaklawn, and for the next hour she reviewed all the things they'd done. When her mind turned toward home, she said, "I almost dread to go home and see what has happened at Oaklawn. I still have my harasser to worry about!"

"We'll work to solve that right away," he said. "I don't know enough about your neighbors to know who might be harassing you. It might be some member of the Cooper family. I didn't like the looks of some of the cousins who came to the wedding. Maybe it's one of them. I've even wondered if it could be Kevin."

"He's always been helpful. I can't believe he'd torment me like that. There has been some talk about the college expanding its borders—maybe some developer is trying to drive me away so he could make a lot of money if that happens."

"What about the Howes? They're around your place a lot."

"It isn't them," Laurel said stubbornly.

"Well, I don't think they're involved, either. There has to be a connection between your harassment and the offer to buy Oaklawn. Perhaps you can coerce Kevin into telling you who the potential buyer is."

"He can be awfully stubborn."

"But if you tell him about your harassment, he might relent. At any rate, the next time you have a note or phone call, you should contact the police. In the meantime, there are more important things to take care of."

Micah took the ring he'd bought in Caracas from his pocket. "Don't you think it's time you started wearing this? I want to get married before my duties start at the college, so we can go on a honeymoon. And you should have the thrill of being engaged a while before we're married."

Even though she'd promised to marry Micah, she briefly thought of all the reasons she shouldn't marry him. She still had a mystery hanging over her head. And what if, after they were married, Micah couldn't be happy settled down in one place? Would she want to leave Oaklawn? If she got married, how would that change her relationship with Debbie? But annoyed at herself, Laurel decided it was time for her to listen to her heart instead of her mind.

She lifted her left hand toward Micah. "I don't want to get married at Oaklawn," she said.

"Neither do I," he confirmed with an engaging smile.

"In fact, I'm not even keen on living there, but I know it's the sensible thing to do. If you want to keep the place for Debbie, it can't stand empty. I'll accept Oaklawn as long as you go with it."

Micah slipped the ring on her finger. Not really caring what their fellow passengers thought, he leaned over and kissed her. "I love you, Laurel."

"And I love you. I'll always be grateful to God for sending you my way at a time when I needed you so much."

"If I live with you at Oaklawn, will you travel with

me part of the time? I'm not ready to settle down yet. Or do you still want to get a college education?"

"Couldn't I do both?"

"No reason you can't. You can go to school while I'm teaching, and we can travel the rest of the time. You'll get an education traveling, too."

"This wonderful trip with you has taught me that I like to travel. But not all the time. I like to be home."

"Where do you want to go on our honeymoon?" Micah asked.

"Paris," she said without hesitation. "But maybe I shouldn't ask for anything that expensive. This trip has cost you a lot."

"No problem. I don't have vast wealth like Kenneth Morrow, but I can afford a few trips every year. I'm paid well for my assignments. And I own some good wheat land in Kansas. In addition to receiving income from the sale of grain, there are three abundant oil wells on the land. I can afford a honeymoon in Paris."

While they waited for their luggage at the airport, Laurel called to let Johnny Sizemore, the tenant who'd been living in her house, know they would be home in about an hour. "You can go on to your apartment if you want to."

"Mrs. Cooper," he blurted out. "I'd better stay. There was a break-in while you were gone, and I don't like to leave the house."

"What kind of a break-in? Did they take anything?"

"I don't know that much about your home. You'll have to decide when you get here."

"When did this happen?"

"Two nights ago. I usually have a night class on Wednesday, but it was canceled, so I came home earlier than usual. I surprised somebody in the basement. He ran away when I came in."

"We'll be there soon," Laurel said.

"Maybe I should have called the cops, but I didn't know what to do."

Micah was lifting their suitcases from the carousel when she went back to him.

"What's happened now?" he asked, always alert to her concerns.

She told him what Johnny had said. "I'd hoped we would have a little reprieve when we came home."

"Well, I've had enough. We're going to find out what's going on. Do you want to go to the police?"

"I think it's time. I'll call as soon as I see what damage has been done."

But although Laurel and Micah searched every room in the house, they couldn't find anything missing. The basement was a mess, however, because the intruder had moved the cabinets and taken items from the shelves and thrown them on the floor. Boxes were overturned. And a shovel was leaning against the wall in the fruit cellar.

"That shovel isn't mine," Laurel said.

"What is the man looking for?" Micah said. "Buried treasure?"

"You might not be so far wrong at that. You remember I told you about the family legend that silver and gold was hidden on the estate before the Union army invaded the South. My father-in-law made light of the story, so I didn't believe it, either."

"But if someone has heard that legend, they might be looking for the treasure. Let's not notify the police yet. Maybe we can set a trap for your burglar. I'll put security cameras on each floor of the house and see what we can learn. If there's any other way, I don't want you exposed to a lot of publicity."

By Express Mail, Laurel sent Debbie the ten-page letter she'd started in Caracas and had finished on the plane. She wanted Debbie to know about Jason before anyone else learned it. Debbie telephoned as soon as she'd read the letter.

"Mom," she said, "your letter was almost like the stories you made up and told me when I was a child. It's unbelievable—finding Daddy's friend, and that trip into the jungle. Weren't you scared?"

"A little, but it was exciting, too."

"I had a good cry before I called. I know it must have been difficult for you. I wish I could have been there with you."

"I wanted you to be there."

"When will Daddy's remains get to Tennessee?"

"I don't know. Kenneth Morrow will notify us."

"Shouldn't we have a memorial service?"

"Probably so, since there's never been one for him. Your grandparents wouldn't agree to a memorial service, because they couldn't admit their son was dead. I'll talk to Pastor Jensen about it. Maybe we can have one when you and Dereck come here for Thanksgiving or Christmas."

"It was nice of Micah to be so concerned."

"He took some pictures of the cemetery, and he'll send them to you on e-mail." Taking a deep breath, she said, "You should see the diamond ring he bought for me. We're going to get married."

Debbie squealed, and she said to Dereck, "Mom and Micah are going to get married!"

Laurel heard Dereck say, "Great news!" before Debbie said to her mother, "That's awesome! Have you set the date?"

"No. Would you be offended if we go away by ourselves to get married? I'm not in the mood for another big wedding right now."

"I won't mind. I'm not sure I want to watch you get married anyway. I like Micah and want you to marry him, but it still hurts a little to know you won't be completely mine anymore."

Laurel laughed. "Then you know how I felt the day you got married."

Chapter Sixteen

After she said goodbye to Debbie, Laurel wondered if she would ever tell her daughter about the disturbing summer she'd had. If Micah and she could solve the mystery, she might tell her, but it depended on who was involved.

When Micah and Laurel attended church the first Sunday after their return, her friends quickly spotted the diamond ring. The newly engaged couple refused to tell when they were going to get married, but Laurel finally said, "We're going to elope, so don't plan on attending the wedding."

Micah had suggested that they could be married at one of the chapels in Gatlinburg, and she'd agreed. But they didn't want to get married until they tried to solve the mystery surrounding Oaklawn. They made their plans carefully.

Since they'd hinted at an elopement, when Laurel

told Pete and Brenda they were going to be away for two or three days, Brenda jumped to the conclusion that they were going to get married. Laurel didn't correct her friend. And because Micah considered Kevin a possible suspect, she also called to tell him she would be gone. She'd been somewhat amused at how affably Kevin had congratulated her on her upcoming marriage. He certainly didn't seem sad that she'd refused *his* offer and yet was marrying another man.

A week after they'd returned from Venezuela, late one evening, they drove to the Knoxville Airport and turned in Micah's rental car. After Micah determined that no one had followed them, they took a taxi to within a mile of Oaklawn.

"I can't see a thing," Laurel said after the taxi drove away, and they started walking through the dense woods that separated Oaklawn from the highway. Although Micah said that they should use their flashlights sparingly, the night was dark, and after she stumbled a few times, Laurel kept hers on until the house was in sight.

"I feel like a burglar," she whispered to Micah when they came to the house and she unlocked the back door.

"Don't leave the key in its normal hiding place," he advised. "If someone does break in, at least we'll know they weren't using your key."

Their plan to catch the prowler was very simple. Micah would sleep in the basement, and if the prowler came, he would alert Laurel by pulling on a small rope they'd run through a hole where the telephone service came into the living room. That would be her cue to come to the top of the stairs and turn on the basement light. Micah planned to tackle the culprit and keep him captive until they called the authorities.

Earlier in the day, Micah had prepared a cot in the basement, and after he kissed Laurel, he went downstairs. Laurel spread some blankets on the couch in the living room. She didn't undress, although she removed her shoes, lay on the couch and tied the rope around her wrist.

Laurel wasn't sleepy and she monitored the passage of time by listening to the clock on the stairway chiming the hour. The last chimes she heard were at two o'clock, and when she awoke, it was daylight.

She crept down the basement steps and whispered, "Micah, are you awake?"

He came out of the furnace room where he'd placed the cot. "I haven't slept at all. I heard imaginary sounds all night. I intend to sleep most of the day in one of your bedrooms—that way, I can stay awake again tonight."

"Do you want to eat breakfast first?"

"I'd rather sleep for a few hours. What are you going to do while I'm sleeping?"

"Probably sit and chew my nails wondering what we'll find out, or if this cloak-and-dagger stuff is useless."

Yawning, he said, "Call me if you have any trouble. Which room shall I take?"

"Why not use Debbie's room? It's the one on the right at the rear of the hallway."

He blew her a kiss. "I probably won't sleep long."

The day seemed endless to Laurel. She couldn't listen to the radio or television. She couldn't turn on any lights, and with the draperies closed, she couldn't even see to read or do needlework. While Micah slept, Laurel spent a lot of time praying. She thanked God for letting her know the truth about Jason's death. She thanked Him for making Debbie the kind of person she was—a daughter who wanted her mother's happiness. And most of all, she was thankful for Micah.

The past two weeks, when they'd been alone so much, he could easily have pressed her into doing things that would have violated her moral values. She'd occasionally discerned flashes of desire in his eyes, but he had treated her as a friend. With two exceptions, she thought whimsically, remembering their emotional embrace after they'd returned from Jason's grave. But by then, they both knew she was free to love again.

About four o'clock, while they were eating sandwiches, a vehicle came along the driveway and parked in front of the portico. Several knocks sounded at the locked front door, and the knob turned. Laurel and Micah exchanged contemplative glances across the kitchen table. Soon the car drove away.

"Wonder who that could have been?" Laurel whispered, for they hadn't dared to look out the windows.

"No way to tell," Micah said softly. "May I take a Thermos of tea to the basement with me?" he asked.

"I'll prepare it for you. There are some cookies in

that cabinet on the far left. You can put some of those on a plate and take them with you."

"I have the feeling we'll have a visitor tonight."

"I hope so. I can't stand this uncertainty and waiting. You seem as calm as ever."

He grinned at her. "You're just naturally impatient. I've learned to wait. Many times, I've waited behind a photographer's blind all day for a wild animal to show up and pose for a perfect picture."

"Well, even if we don't catch our intruder, I hope your cameras will pick up his picture."

His hands filled with the Thermos and plate of cookies, Micah leaned over and kissed her on the forehead before he went downstairs. Darkness came, and Laurel settled down for another night of waiting.

Since she hadn't slept much during the day, still fully clothed except for shoes, Laurel went to sleep early, to be woken by the tightening of the rope on her arm.

She sat up rapidly, and walking softly, she went to the top of the basement steps. She could hear furtive movements below, and she flipped the light switch. Suddenly a tussle ensued in the basement, and although Micah had told her to stay upstairs until he called her, Laurel ran down the steps.

Micah was struggling with a figure draped in a black robe with a black hood over his head. Micah struck his fist at where the man's chin must have been and the struggling ceased. Micah saw Laurel fidgeting beside him, and he motioned her back. Micah grabbed a piece of rope and twisted it several times around the man's middle, binding his arms to his sides. He anchored the rope to the stair banister.

The burglar began to struggle, and Micah said to Laurel, "Shall we have the unveiling?"

Mutely, she nodded.

Standing behind the man, Micah gave a swift tug and pulled the hood off.

Laurel was caught off guard as she looked into the eyes of their burglar. Her body stiffened in shock, and for a moment, she merely stared, tongue-tied.

A bleak, tight-lipped smile spread across Micah's face. He covertly turned on a tape recorder before he moved to confront the man he'd always suspected had the greatest reason to intimidate Laurel. Micah's movement startled Laurel, and her utter astonishment turned to anger.

"Cousin Kevin!" she shouted. "How dare you! How dare you break into this house?"

"I'm more interested in the answer to another question," Micah said. "Why have you been harassing Laurel all summer?"

Angrily and defiantly, Kevin Cooper stared at them and didn't answer.

Micah pointed to the security cameras focused on the scene. "You don't have many choices," he said, "because we have you dead to rights. You have about two minutes to make up your mind. If you don't want to talk to us, I'm calling the police. And we may still call the police even after you talk. We're making no promises."

Kevin stared at Micah, quick anger rising in his eyes. His features hardened, and between clenched teeth, his curt voice lashed at Micah. "I can't see that it's any of your business what I'm doing at Oaklawn."

"It's my business when someone harasses the woman I love."

With a contemptuous shrug, Kevin looked at Laurel, his nostrils flaring with fury. She'd known this man for over twenty-five years, and Laurel had never suspected that such a volatile personality lurked beneath his sophisticated demeanor.

"What do you say, Laurel? Are you going to turn me over to the police just because you found me in the cellar? Truth to tell, this estate belongs to me more than you. I'm Jason's nearest male relative, and my uncle told me he wanted me to have Oaklawn."

Laurel's temper flared, and she said, "What you're doing tonight comes second to some other things I want to know. Why have you been calling and sending those intimidating notes?"

"Prove it," he said maliciously. "I'd like to see you prove it."

Laurel glanced sideways at Micah, and he shook his head slightly. She didn't know what his signal meant, but her temper was in control now, and she stormed, "I don't have to prove it, but I'm sure that once you're locked up in jail, the phone calls will cease. And as for Micah, we're getting married, and we'll be living at Oaklawn, so if he asks you a question, answer it."

Kevin squirmed around in his ropes, and Micah knew the man was uncomfortable, but he wouldn't untie his bonds yet. Kevin might be armed, and he wasn't taking any chance on Laurel being hit by a bullet.

Laurel moved to confront him. "And you tried to kill Debbie!"

She lifted a hand to slap his face, but Micah caught her hand, as Kevin protested, "I had nothing to do with that. Do you think I'd hurt her?"

"You've tried to steal her inheritance. Why wouldn't I suspect you?"

"I didn't do it!"

Laurel didn't know if he was telling the truth, but she'd prefer to believe that the man she'd trusted for so long wasn't guilty of attempted murder.

"As for proving you've been tormenting Laurel this summer," Micah said, "it won't be difficult to trace it to you. We'd have done it before, but Laurel didn't want any scandal before Debbie's wedding." He turned to Laurel. "Watch him, but keep your distance so he can't kick you. I'm going to take this shovel and dig in the fruit cellar and see if I can find what he's been looking for. That's the only earthen floor in this basement."

Micah turned so he was facing Kevin and Laurel, who both watched his every move. Kevin watched in rage, Laurel with anticipation.

Micah picked up a three-foot-long quarter-inch pipe that he'd leaned against the wall earlier in the day. He started pounding the pipe into the ground. His first four soundings went easily into the solid earth, but on the next try, when he had driven the pipe a foot, a crushing sound reached their ears.

"Stop! Stop!" Kevin said. "You're ruining priceless artifacts."

Micah flashed a look of triumph toward Laurel. Lazily, he came out of the cellar and smiled sardonically at Kevin.

"How do you know?"

"My arms are going to sleep tied up like this. Untie me, and I'll tell you."

"You tell us, and then we'll talk about turning you loose," Laurel said. "To think that you've pretended to be my friend and have been so deceitful. Advising me to borrow more money than I could afford to, thinking I'd get so far in debt that I'd have to sell Oaklawn. When that didn't work, you had the nerve to ask me to marry you so you could get your hands on this property. As far as I'm concerned you can stay tied up."

Knowing Laurel's temper, Micah figured Cousin Kevin would have been better off to trust *his* judgment rather than hers.

"Go ahead and dig, Micah," she said.

"No!" Kevin shouted. "I'll tell you—just don't destroy a lot of things. Can't you at least loosen this rope?"

Micah looked at Laurel and she nodded. But before he loosened the rope, Micah frisked Cousin Kevin, found a gun in his front left pocket, and removed it before he gave Kevin enough slack to sit down on a bench.

"The Cooper gold and silver that disappeared during the Civil War is buried in the cellar."

"I don't believe that," Laurel said. "According to Grandfather Cooper, it was supposed to have been buried in the peach orchard."

"It *was* buried in the orchard, but during Reconstruction, our great-grandfather decided he could keep better watch over it in the house. I found an old diary of his when I was visiting at Oaklawn once, and I borrowed it to read. But I didn't get around to reading it until last winter."

"Why didn't you just come and talk to Debbie and me about it? We would have shared it with the family."

"But Laurel," Micah said, "he wanted *all* of it."

"As the only male Cooper in our family, it should be mine," Kevin said defiantly.

"Laurel, I don't think we should do any digging until we have some witnesses. Let's call the sheriff."

"Yes, it's time. I'll go upstairs and phone."

Micah rewound the video and handed it to her. "Put this in a safe place."

Laurel walked up the stairs assailed by a terrible sense of bitterness. Her anger had faded now, and she was disillusioned by Kevin's deceit.

When she came back downstairs, Kevin, still bound, was lying on a cot staring at the ceiling. Micah met her at the foot of the stairs and they quietly made plans. When he approached Kevin again, Micah said, "The sheriff and his deputy are coming to witness our excavation. Laurel has also called Pete Howe to come and help dig up the treasure."

"We have your confession on tape, but we hope we won't have to use it," Laurel said. "To prevent a family scandal and humiliation to your daughters, we're going to release you. As far as the sheriff or anyone knows, the three of us were searching for the treasure based on what you'd read in that diary. Whether or not we reveal what we've learned about you depends on your future conduct."

Kevin made no comment, and Laurel looked at him pityingly. She motioned for Micah to remove the bonds that held Kevin. She was over her anger, and she was saddened by the end of the friendship with Kevin. She couldn't number how many times he'd visited in this house since she'd been in the family, but she didn't figure he'd ever come again. Even if she forgave him, some breaches couldn't be repaired. Her anticipation of what they'd find in the cellar was tempered by the sadness of the ruined relationship. Debbie had few relatives, and it would hurt her to lose Cousin Kevin and possibly his children, if they ever learned what their father had done.

Pete and Brenda came as soon as Laurel called them. Several other neighbors, who had police scanners and had heard the call for assistance at Laurel's house, had gathered on the portico before the sheriff and his deputy, sirens blazing, drove up. Some had come out of curiosity, others to offer their help. Knowing he would have to get used to the local Pony Express, Micah decided to grin and bear it.

The sheriff ordered the curious neighbors to keep out of the basement. Micah had locked the outside basement door, and the small group involved went through the grand hall and down the inside steps to the basement. After they were on their way, Laurel also locked the other doors so no one would sneak in.

Brenda and Laurel sat on the steps, where they had a good view of the door to the fruit cellar. Pete took off his jacket and worked in T-shirt and jeans, while Micah wore his customary denim shorts and a polo shirt as they attacked the dirt packed down from years of use. The sheriff, his deputy and Cousin Kevin watched from the background. After clearing away two feet of dirt, the men unearthed two badly deteriorated medium-sized trunks. Before they opened the trunks, Micah motioned to Laurel, and she jumped off the steps and hurried to his side.

The sheriff lifted the lids of both trunks and all of the spectators crowded close together to see the treasure. Laurel had figured, if there were any precious items, that after almost a century and a half, nothing would be salvaged. An hour later, she knew she'd been wrong. All of the items had been carefully wrapped and had suffered little damage during their long interment in the ground.

Most of the silver and gold pieces had been imported from Europe, as had the two sets of silver flatware. There were several cups, bowls and plates for infants.

Most of the items were silver, but there were a few gold vases and figurines. Several of the pieces had the Cooper coat-of-arms. Two leather bags were filled with U.S. gold and silver coins, and since they had been minted before 1860, they were valuable indeed.

After the sheriff had tallied all of the items, he said, "Mrs. Cooper, since these items were found in your home, they're yours. What shall I do with them?"

Micah and Laurel had already talked over what to do with anything they found, so she didn't hesitate. "Since these items are undoubtedly priceless, I'd like you to take charge of them and put them in safekeeping. I don't think it's safe for me to keep them at Oaklawn." She didn't glance at Kevin when she said this.

"Maybe I'm asking you to do something not included in your duties," she continued, "but I'd like help in finding a reputable antique dealer or coin collector to look over everything and give me some idea of their worth."

"You can store them in the vault of one of the local banks," the sheriff said. "If you want to sell them, the banks will be glad to handle the sale for a small commission."

Pete and Micah had pitched the dirt back in the hole while Laurel and the sheriff had been talking, and they helped the deputy carry the articles to the car. The sheriff had looked curiously at Kevin several times during the morning, obviously wondering why he was so silent.

When Laurel, Cousin Kevin and the sheriff were left

alone in the basement, wanting a witness to her proposal to Kevin, Laurel said, "Cousin Kevin, since these are Cooper heirlooms, I don't want any of them. I will contact Debbie to get her approval, but if she agrees, after we get an estimate on the worth of the treasure, I'll talk to Debbie. The items can be divided between Debbie and your daughters. If she wants to sell her share, you can give me a check for half of the value, which I'll put in a trust fund for Debbie and her children. If your daughters and Debbie want to keep the heirlooms, we'll divide the items, share and share alike, with one half for them, the other half for Debbie."

The expression on Kevin's face hadn't changed at all, and again the sheriff eyed him in astonishment.

"Do you think that solution is fair, Kevin?" Laurel asked.

After clearing his throat several times, Kevin said, "Yes, very fair."

The sheriff, in his booming voice, said, "I think it's more than fair, because you're not obligated to give anyone else any of this booty."

Kevin shook hands with Laurel, saying quietly, "Thank you. I'll be in touch after you hear from the antique dealers." The remorse in his eyes saddened Laurel, and she was glad she hadn't had to reveal Kevin's evil actions.

"Don't expect to see much of me during the next month," she said. "I'm getting married and going on honeymoon."

Micah paused at the top of the stairs, his pulse quickening at her words. He turned and walked to the portico where they bade goodbye to the police officers, Kevin, the Howes and the curious neighbors, who went home happy, having heard the story of the buried treasure from Pete.

Laurel and Micah spent the rest of the day restoring the basement to order. After they finished, Micah went to his apartment to check his e-mail and to take care of some correspondence. If Laurel planned to be married and return from their honeymoon within a month, there was a lot to be done.

They met again on the portico later that evening. The sunset was gorgeous, and its rays painted the river crimson as it meandered down the broad valley. She greeted him with a shy smile, and her lashes dropped before his compelling eyes.

"I heard you tell the sheriff and Kevin that you were going to be married soon. Am I invited to the wedding?"

"Unless you're having second thoughts about giving me this?" she retorted, waving her ring finger under his nose.

"No second thoughts," he said, pulling her loosely into his arms. "Shall I call one of the chapels in Gatlinburg and make arrangements? They'll provide everything—tux, wedding dress, flowers and whatever."

She laughed up into his eyes. "I don't want a formal wedding, and I know you wouldn't like it. I suppose we would need witnesses, though."

"Let's ask Pete and Brenda to drive over with us," Micah suggested. "I'll make reservations for our trip to Paris as soon as we set the date."

With all of the hectic things that had happened this summer, it seemed as if she had known Micah a lifetime, but now that the moment had arrived for her to become his wife, Laurel's heartbeat skyrocketed.

Micah's eyes were full of love and tenderness, and she reached up to cradle his cheek. "I love you, Micah. God willing, I pray we'll have many happy years together."

He hugged her to him, and kissed her again and again. As she returned his kisses, she rejoiced in his strength and the certainty that he returned her love. He released her. She moved to the edge of the portico and looked out over Oaklawn's broad fields. She'd had many troubles and disappointments here, but also lots of happiness. Laurel looked forward to marrying Micah, but her joy was tempered with nostalgia. Silently she said goodbye to her life with Jason, her in-laws and Debbie. Micah was her future, and she wouldn't have it any other way.

Sensing her mood, Micah stood behind her, put his arms around her waist and kissed the curls at her neckline. He listened to his heart and was overwhelmed with peace and satisfaction. What a difference four months had made! He glanced over Oaklawn's fields and happiness filled his heart. He was at home.

Five days later, Laurel and Micah, accompanied by the Howes, drove down a secluded country lane to a rustic log chapel at Gatlinburg. Micah wore a dark blue suit, white shirt and a blue striped tie. Laurel had chosen to be married in the dress she'd bought for Debbie's wedding. Micah had a white rose boutonniere, and she carried a mixed bouquet of roses.

Organ music swelled softly around them as Micah and Laurel took their places at the altar. They had asked for a short ceremony, and after the minister prayed and read a few Scripture verses concerning marriage, he took their vows.

"Micah Davidson, forsaking all others, do you take this woman, whom you hold by the hand, to be your lawful wedded wife, to have and to hold, from this day forward, for better, for worse, for richer, for poorer, in sickness and in health, to love and to cherish as long as you both shall live?"

Waiting for his reply, Laurel looked sweet and obedient, and smothering a grin, Micah remained silent. Still looking angelic, Laurel slanted a quick look at him, but Micah didn't meet her eyes.

"Mr. Davidson," the preacher prompted, "you're supposed to respond, 'I do.'"

Again Micah hesitated, and the minister peered over his glasses at him. When he started to speak again, Micah held up his hand.

"I heard you, but I'm considering. This is a pretty serious vow. I want to think it over."

Pete smothered a snort. Brenda gasped. Laurel turned on Micah, seething with anger and humiliation.

"Thinking it over! Micah, how dare you," she said and hit him on the chest with her bouquet. She lifted her eyes to his and saw that they brimmed with mirth. His lips trembled as he tried to control his laughter, which incensed her even more.

She hit him again with the flowers and rose petals flew in all directions.

"You did that on purpose, just to make me mad."

Laughing aloud, he said, "I couldn't resist the temptation. The first day we met you got angry at me. Why not be angry on our wedding day?"

Laurel's anger faded as fast as it had flashed. She shook her head. Life with this unpredictable man would never be dull. Clasping her hand again, Micah turned to face the minister.

"Yes, I'll take her," he said, "Temper and all."

* * * * *

Dear Reader,

As I finished the fifth and final book in my MELLOW YEARS series, I've reflected on the writing of these books and the response I've had to them.

The idea for the series was born in the year 2000 when I first discussed it with my Steeple Hill editor. It has taken four years to bring the full series to fruition. I've worked with five different editors on the publication of these books.

The books are unique, in that the heroes and heroines are all in their forties. A large number of my readers fall into that age group, and have been able to identify with the struggles of my characters, yet my younger readers have also liked the books. I've received a lot of mail about the series, but one letter that encouraged me to know that my hard work is appreciated came from a reader concerning *Love at Last,* the first book in the series.

In part, that letter said, "Your book blessed me. The Holy Spirit ministered to me, and I know that regardless, God loves me. Thanks for the encouragement to stand firm. Not everyone can be preachers, preaching from a pulpit, but you are indeed a preacher—preaching through your books."

Writing is hard work, but it's worthwhile when I know that my books encourage those who read them.

In His name,

Irene B. Brand

Love Inspired

UNDERCOVER BLESSINGS

BY

DEB KASTNER

Returning to her childhood home was the only way Lily Montague could keep her injured child safe—little Abigail had witnessed a friend's kidnapping and was in danger. Kevin MacCormack, called "guardian angel" by the girl, was helping her daughter learn to walk again. But Lily didn't know the strong but gentle man was an undercover FBI agent, there to protect them both. When his secret was revealed, would it destroy the fragile bond that had formed between them?

Don't miss

UNDERCOVER BLESSINGS
On sale January 2005

Available at your favorite retail outlet.

A MOTHER FOR CINDY

BY

MARGARET DALEY

Widow Jesse Bradshaw had her hands full with her young son, her doll-making business and a gaggle of pets. She couldn't imagine adding anything more to her already crowded life—until jaded Nick Blackburn and his daughter moved in next door. Jesse was all set to use her matchmaking skills to find a mate for the workaholic widower, but what would she do when she realized that she wanted to be little Cindy's mom?

THE LADIES OF SWEETWATER LAKE:
Like a wedding ring, this circle of friends is never ending.

Don't miss

A MOTHER FOR CINDY
On sale January 2005

Available at your favorite retail outlet.

www.SteepleHill.com   LIAMFCMD

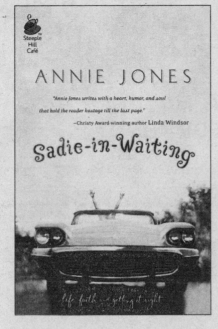

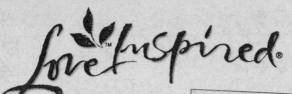

TO HEAL A HEART

BY

ARLENE JAMES

Finding a handwritten letter at the airport offering forgiveness to an unknown recipient put widowed lawyer Mitch Sayer on a quest to uncover its addressee...until he sat down next to Piper Wynne. His lovely seatmate made him temporarily forget his mission. After the flight, he kept running into Piper, whose eyes hid painful secrets...including the fact that the letter was written to her!

Don't miss

TO HEAL A HEART
On sale January 2005

Available at your favorite retail outlet.

Love Came Unexpectedly

BY

Ruth Scofield

Inheriting a fishing resort from her grandfather
wasn't something Sunny Merrill had ever expected—
she'd been orphaned at a young age and hadn't ever
met the man. Always there to lend a hand was neighbor
Grant Prentiss, the handsome rancher and riding stable
owner who knew a lot about Sunshine Acres. Yet their
unexpected love was threatened by a secret Grant
was keeping from her....

Don't miss

LOVE CAME UNEXPECTEDLY
On sale January 2005

Available at your favorite retail outlet.